World

A Novel

Jane Barr

WORLD

Copyright ©2025 Jane Barr

Paperback ISBN   978-0-473-74261-4
Epub ISBN 978-0-473-74263-8
Hardback ISBN 978-0-473-74263-8

Jane Barr Books
www.Janebarrbooks.com

To Duncan

"World" is a fictional story
inspired by true events

*"I am not an Athenian,
or a
Greek,
but a citizen of the world."*

(Socrates)

People in this Book

The Macedonians (first part)
Andronicus of Macedonia, son of a small arms
maker
Idahlia of Macedonia, wife of Andronicus
Leo of Macedonia, former court poet
Alexander, Macedonia King
Hephaestion. Alexander's best friend and a general
in his army

The Sogdians
Baron Oxyartes. Warlord of the north of Persia
Muni formerly of the northern steppes. Baron
Oxyartes wife
Leila formerly of Sagartia. Baron Oxyartes wife
Roxane. Leila's daughter
Shapur. Muni's son
Bah, Oxyartes Brother.
Fahr, Bah's son.

The Travellers
Phaidros of Ithaca
Zek of many places

More Macedonians (all Generals in the army)
Peucestas, boyhood friend of Alexander.
Craterus, boyhood friend of Alexander, also known
as the strongest
Ptolemy, lover of Thais
Perdicass
Antipater. Left to take care of the homeland in
Alexander's absence
Cassander, Antipater's son

Assistants
Sarah of the Bactrian Court
Nico of Macedonia, manservant

Courtesans
Thais and Omphale

The Babylonians
Beulah, the dressmaker and Benjamin her son

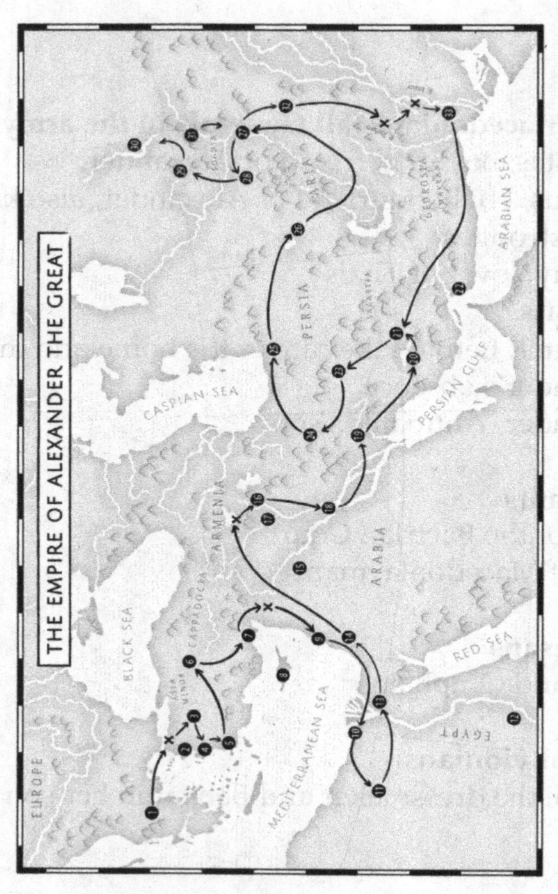

THE EMPIRE OF ALEXANDER THE GREAT
EUROPE
BLACK SEA
CASPIAN SEA
MEDITERRANEAN SEA
EGYPT
RED SEA
ARABIA
ARABIAN SEA
PERSIAN GULF
PERSIA
ARMENIA
CAPPADOCIA
ASIA MINOR

Places

X Important Battles
Major Cities

1	Pella
2	Troy
3	Sardis
4	Ephesus
5	Halicarnassus
6	Gordium
7	Tarsus
8	Paphos
9	Tyre
10	Alexandria
11	Amun
12	Abu Simbel
13	Memphis
14	Jerusalem
15	Tadmor
16	Arbela
17	Nineveh
18	Babylon
19	Susa
20	Persepolis
21	Pasargadae
22	Salmous
23	Gabae
24	Ecbatana
25	Hecatompylos
26	Artacana
27	Alexandria in Cauaso
28	Bactria
29	Samarkand
30	Tashkent
31	Sogdian Rock
32	Taxila
33	Patala

Table of Contents

Asia Minor 334 BC

I hold Idahlia high upon my shoulders as we reach the shores of Asia Minor. She is light, my Idahlia; lean, and as tall as the willow that touches the stream's edge here at the southern end of the coast.

She has no sorrow. It is I who holds the sadness fast within my soul. And it is in my dreams that my mother comes to me, her cheeks wet with tears as she holds out the tiny copper pot. They spill onto its side and turn the copper green. It is the pot I crafted for her as a small boy—an apprentice piece my father insisted I make. And now it rests inside another piece, also made as a test. My wooden box, created to show my father I was as good with wood as I was with metal. On its lid I carved the faces of the three Fates, their long braids curving against the sides, softening the hard look of the cedarwood.

When I wake from these dreams I shiver, and my father's words fill me: *We make small arms—the sharpest knives and daggers and swords.* He coughs, as he always coughs. The smoke of the indoor forge lies deep in his lungs after many years bent over his work. And then his words spin in the dusty dawn of our tent: *We have a duty, my son, to keep supplying the kingdom. It matters not that the young fool of a king takes his feet and our army out of our well-kept lands. We must remain strong and deliver our arms to those who need them. We protect those loyal to Phillip.*

Idahlia buries her soft, dark-brown hair into my shoulders and kisses my neck and my hands. We both hold the small grey pebbles that litter this shore. Our legs are still wet from the passage through the strait where the salty water licked our thighs, and our cart became like a small boat. I collect small pieces of driftwood and kindle a fire. I am good at building fires. I learnt how to do this from my father, who learnt from his father.

I repeat his words to Idahlia: "*A well-tended flame kept at the heat needed to melt metal has within its heart the power of Apollo. Apollo with Hephaestus looks over us. Guards us from those with ill intent.*"

The initial excitement of the travel, the camaraderie, the convivial disposition of those who walk behind and in front of us has waned, for the line is hierarchal. Hierarchy was something my father detested. I have observed the line: the military, then the courtesans, then the rest of us, who jostle for position.

It has become apparent that we must fend for ourselves. And our supplies are limited. In our box on which the Fates bow is just one bag of gold. When I begin to imagine the sanctuary of home—for that is what that bag of gold could buy, safe passage home, leaving this uncertainty behind—I also see my father's wrath. I feel it, for he threw that bag of gold at my feet as Idahlia and I left his gates.

Idahlia finds me and drags me from the log that I rest on. She smells of the sea. Our fire blazes and warms us. We both look out to the horizon as the waves of Asia Minor curl in and out, sounding like a wind that is wild on a night draped in clouds. Idahlia has crumbs on her lips. I stare at them.

"Oh yes, see that man there," she says. "Well, when he wasn't looking, I snatched the bread off his plate."

I take her hand as we walk back to our modest tent. From our cart I take a flask of wine. I pour a cup.

"Take it to the man you took the bread from."

She looks at me aghast and shakes her head. I take it and the man is grateful. I do not mention the missing bread. He tells me that tomorrow it is likely we will move towards Troy. The man says he is turning back. This life is not for him.

The day has slipped away. A poet named Leo sits beside us. He gives us some relief; the walking tests me and this entertaining and jocular man takes my mind off the blisters that paste my feet.

"Andronicus," he says in his burly voice, "that noise you hear, it is not my bowels. My bowels play tunes regularly. Very good tunes, but tonight it is my stomach. It growls like a randy lion."

We have no food left but we do have wine. I pour him a small measure, for that too is running low.

"I wish I had never consented to follow him." Leo says. His face is scarred from years of troubled skin, his lips cracked from his time under the sun.

"Did he ask you to follow him?" Idahlia says.

"Yes, he did. Asked me one evening—well, he did not directly ask. He rather said something like, 'My dear, old friend Leo. Always at my side. Mocked by my father but cherished by me.'" Leo pauses. He mimics the King's accent well. He clears his throat. "He said to me, he did, my dear Idahlia, 'Old man, I cannot live without your humour, your vulgarity and your insolent language; the way you can tell stories in the voices of men and women both foreign and native.'"

Idahlia begins her own act. I am reluctant to acknowledge this, but with each telling her tale grows into something I imagine is far from the truth. From the old washerwoman who saved her to the dressing of the King's mother, she adds and folds in more and more astonishing detail. I am loathe to say it, but I believe much of it is plucked from her own mind, rather like a child picks a flower.

"Oh, Leo, you know how I dressed Olympias in the finest silk and poured scent over her like wine?"

"Well, all that happened behind the well-guarded door of Olympias—shall we call her Evil Olympias? She had terrible taste in pets, as we all know." Leo says.

They continue with this banter, Leo neither refuting her tales nor confirming them.

I look down the beach where we have settled for the night. Local fishermen are repairing nets and drinking something that has made them jolly. They sit cross-legged around their own fire. I wander over to them. I have a silver ring that I found in the dirt on our travels today—collecting things takes my mind off the monotony of travel and the dirt that gets in my sandals, causing those blisters.

I see a basket full of their catch, wrapped in wet cloth, ready for market. I offer them the ring. One of the men nods towards the freshly caught fish. He rises and hands over five fish.

I fry up the fish in the little bit of olive oil that I have.

"Here, Andronicus, man of fire and metal—place one of them good fish on my plate." Leo wipes his mouth with the sleeve of his chiton; he has already eaten two of the fillets. Now he wants a third. I eye him up, but he winks at me and then laughs.

"It's not for me, good chap." he says.

He leaves us to consort with a fine redhead who is paddling at the shore. But neither Leo nor the fish can tempt her. She turns her back on him and wades further out into the ocean. I wonder if she too is having second thoughts about following the young King into these lands. He called them new lands; lands of prosperity and wealth, of abundance and bounty. He described to us on that first day of the march how we were going to find the golden coast, a paradise, and we would never regret this. That the lands he takes will be ours to share, and riches await all those that follow.

Leo returns. "Worth a try," he says, as he sits his large, bulbous bottom on the log next to the fire. Idahlia laughs and asks him to tell us once more about the night King Phillip was murdered.

He stands and breathes in, closes his eyes and begins his tale of that woeful night.

" He was covered in scars, was our Phillip. Not one patch of his skin had not been sliced open by the tip of a knife and yet none of those wounds had killed him. Our King Phillip whom we loved had been born with the gold-tipped tongue, able to convince any foe to bow down before him and trade and capitulate. And then a spurned lover came out of the docile crowd before him. A much-trusted man; his beloved Pausanias. But he had overlooked him once too often and the young Pausanias came with pockets that jingled, and a knife hidden in his chiton. And so, as the wine warms and the conversation becomes loud, the former lover steps forward and they embrace. As they hold each other Pausanias plunges his sharp knife deep into Phillip's chest—a knife probably made by your father, Andronicus. Think of that. The blade you might have sharpened yourself. The weapon used to assassinate a most valued and adored King."

Andronicus and his father had thought back to that batch of orders. Ptolemy's and Hephaestion's had been among them, the rest were for lower-ranking military men.

But they could not connect the blade to their forge.

Old Leo belches. He asks for pardon, laughs, then staggers forward as if struck by that very knife. "Phillip dies, and the court is sombre. His body lies large and bleeding on the floor of the very court he built up and from where he managed all the Greek states which had come now together in a sort of stable peace."

He is puffed from his narration, and Idahlia places her long arm around his shoulders as he sits once again on the old driftwood log.

"Do you believe the rumour that Olympias was behind the killing?" She asks. The rumour has never been refuted or confirmed.

"Plain and simple, a spurned lover would hold such passion within his soul. Enough to kill his King, but why not kill his latest lover?" Leo muses. "A much younger and prettier version of himself. Yet, one must state that the one to gain the most was of course Olympias, whose status was eroding by the day. As each new child of Phillip's new wife, Cleopatra, who was Macedonian and not of foreign blood, came into being, there was a risk that Alexander, the heir apparent, could lose his spot."

"I don't think she did it," Idahlia says, "for Alexander was always first in line. She told us quite clearly. She made Alexander sit with his father even though he did not care for his company. She would have him tell her all the tales of the court. There was no need to kill Phillip. He would die eventually; he was old and worn."

Leo laughs again. He winks and opens his mouth wide before he speaks. "But who is King today? Who did not waste any time in getting rid of the competition? Who threw poor Cleo's youngest child into a brazier?" He drinks some more of the pilfered wine he and Idahlia snatched today.

I leave them to their banter, their storytelling. They have inveigled some more poor unfortunate travellers—the baggagers, as we are called now—into their lair.

From stability and security to frivolity and folly. That is how my father described the change in the crown. I wander out on the small sandy patch of beach which frames the campsite. I forage and hunt for anything that will augment our standing. Food, primarily. I amass kindle en route, placing the sticks and salvage in the basket I carry upon my back, and I scrutinise the soils, the path, the beaches, searching for any tiny speck of something valuable that I can store in my wooden box.

As my fingers rake through the salty sand, I take my time examining it. The silty coarse grains are so different from those in the little bay that sits below our green hill at home. I smell them. Blood and salt. I filter them through my fingers. I try to see them not as waste, or dust, or washed-up uselessness, but as tiny gems. And when I take them back to the gathering around our good fire, I watch them fall like glitter; gossamer threads. But what is glass, if not melted sand?

Troy 334 BC

Idahlia and Leo hang off every word that comes our way; the gossip, the predictions, the assumptions. The more shocking it is they happier they are.

"Oh, they hanged him—did you know?" one scruffy, odorous man tells us. His red nose runs slick with yellow mucous and his hands are chafed and weeping. My own hands and arms are scarred and marked from burns and cuts, but his hands are riddled with arthritis.

The man does not wait for a response. He bobs his head up and down and continues, "He stole from the soldiery, yes, that's what he did, and he swung like a monkey."

I listen to everyone. But I say nothing. I wait for some kind of information that might put us in a better position. *Find the purpose and prosper, my son. Find the beauty in all that you do, for in that place you will find joy and peace.* But it evades me. I have a forge that is mobile in which I can make things out of what I might find. But we have not stopped long enough for me to engage in what is me. And besides, the voices bring us news. Tell us of how Alexander either raids, or *borrows*, as he calls it, whatever he needs from the willing locals.

In Troy there are good streams to fill our water vessels. I
discover shellfish, and a lone earring wedged in the
crease of a rock. I dig up a coin—a gold coin from
Phillip's reign. His eight-pointed star is etched on one
side, his face on the other. And that evening we eat the
local bitter greens that I have picked and the fat little
lobsters that inhabit the pools on the shore.

Alexander addresses us. He has not done so since
we left Pella. He mounts a rock and stands for some time.
At last the crowd quietens and he begins.

"My mother, as you well know, was descended
from the line of Achilles, my father from the line of
Heracles. We stand here today reverent on this sacred
site, where my ancestor Achilles and his great friend
Patroclus died." He turns to Hephaestion, and then back
again to his people. "This is the place, my friends, where
the Greeks outwitted the Trojans. Like our people before
us we will be victorious in these lands we are about to
enter. The Persians are complacent. They have become
too large and too arrogant. They think they are invincible
just as the Trojans did back then. They have become
comfortable—too comfortable—and they are much
indulged. We will bring them new ways that will make
their people strong and quick witted. Not lazy or stupid.
One day they will thank us for educating their men, for
making them into fine soldiers, for taking the trading
routes from the deceiving and thieving Arabians. We will
become a superior race. The Macedonians, the united
peoples of Greece, will conquer and rule the world."

Alexander pauses, drinks some wine and then
pours a libation out onto the soil. "For my father Zeus."
There is a silence we all know well, the result of how
Alexander now refers to Zeus as his father. Old Leo told
us that this recent addition to his genealogy came after the
extinction of his remaining family (except for poor old
Arridhaeus, who of course will never be King due to his

———

deformities). And it is said, as old Leo reminded us, that Olympias revealed to him one night that a lightning bolt entered her womb and put the seal of the lion on her cervix. And then the son of Zeus was born unto her.

Alexander pours oil onto the soil below. He drinks more from his large silver cup. He then looks at us. "I tell you my friends, my people who follow me hoping for a better life, I tell you my fine troops and Generals and those closest to me, my bodyguards, that have faith and with this in our hands, with the power of Zeus above us, we will fight with honour and we will give gifts to these lands. For it is us, and only us, who have moulded what we have mastered into something more tangible that can be used to advance all mankind. This kind of action has come with great sacrifice. And because of that we must continue with wisdom. With cunning, with bravery. I wish each and every one of you well; I hope that you will take these words and dine on them. That you will be resolute in the fact that you will reach great heights. I pour wine now for the great Achilles who died here, for his friend Patroclus and for the great Heracles in whose footsteps we follow. And now I would ask my seer and dear friend Aristander to read for us."

I do not stay to witness the slaying of a dog whose organs will be examined for good portents. I am anxious to step out on the wild sands of this place and discover what may lie in wait for me.

Idahlia and Leo return joyous.

"The King served wine," Idahlia says. "Now tell me, tell me Leo, Andronicus, how can a woman be so beautiful that a war is fought over her?"

I take out the piece of sea glass that I found on the shore. It is a soft blue.

"Imagine." Idahlia continues when neither of us replies. "Andronicus." She turns to address me front on. With her hands on her hips, she smirks at me. "Would you fight for me if someone came and stole me away?"

I replace the sea glass in my pocket. "If you were kidnapped against your will, yes, I would."

Idahlia turns her back on me. "Leo, would you?" she says to the old entertainer, the former court poet. His red-stained lips open and close. "Well, my dear, you belong to someone else, not to me."

Idahlia sits down and begins to plait her long hair. She has workers' fingers, hands; like mine. Hands that tell of toil and pain. I feel pity for her. In that minute my heart becomes weak. But still I cannot speak of saving her, for if she chose another, would I want to fight for her? I would feel anger, the very thought of it makes me angry now. But angry enough to fight? To defend her honour? In the moment, yes, I would defend her honour if some brute should take her.

In these last moments of the day Apollo's rays warm us and the sea settles a little. The Greeks to me needed the act of kidnap as an excuse to invade Troy.

I look at my wife's face, defeated, for I did not speak the words she wanted to hear.

I walk over and put my arm around her. She touches my face. "You saved me once," she says.

"You saved yourself." I reply.

"The old washerwoman saved my life. After being left on her doorstop to be placed in a boiling pot where she was to make utensils from the baby's bones, she did spare my life."

I nod. "Yes, she saved you. She gave a life of laundering at first and then made you into a fine seamstress."

"She sold me, Andronicus. She sold me to the court, for my stitch was perfect. You would never sell me, would you?"

"No, I would never sell you." That I did know. I would never sell her, nor any person. *No man belongs to another man. A man, a woman, a child, is a soul born to the world and in that world that soul should be free to find what they are called to do.* These words are from my mother, for even though she cried when we left, she told me to follow my heart.

That evening Idahlia begins to tell the story of her birth and her salvation. She tells the group that gathers around our campsite, in front of the good fire, about the washerwoman who didn't throw her in the pot as her mother might have wanted, to erase the birth from all time and to find in the remaining bones a good use. No, the old washerwoman saw something in her. Idahlia tells how she fed her well and taught her all about her business. It was lucrative business—the old washerwoman had all the potions and powders to make a chiton sparkling white. For is white not the colour of power and purity? To wear robes of white that dazzle is nothing short of perfection. She tells her growing band of followers that she would not reveal the secrets that made the washerwoman's garments so white, but she would tell them of her repairs. "My invisible stitch. My stitch so perfect."

One of the group asks her about the babies—were the unwanted still left on the stoop?

She nods. Very unfortunate. But what lives would they have had, some born with a deformity, some born weak, some born with no way to thrive in the world. So they would be sacrificed. Yes, sacrificed to make the cauldron complete, so that the offering of what they left behind could be made into pieces so beautiful. So fanciful, so absurd. They would become valuable talismans that held special magic.

I listen to her. She is beautiful in this role. Leo sits near her and applauds. His quips are not mean, or distasteful. They are playful.

"Young lady of the court of Macedonia, tell us about the snakes that Olympias calls friends."

"Oh yes, the snakes. Well …" Idahlia pauses, a smile on her lips; she drinks wine that someone in the group has brought with them. "She loves those snakes. They serve many purposes, mainly to keep her safe, for many are so frightened of snakes they will not come near her. She is from Epirus, you know? A princess. And that is why many despise her. Because she is foreign. She wears the snakes as jewellery. Imagine this, the emerald-green colour of her favourite snake, Apero, hanging from her neck, complementing her dark-green gown. She does not wear the chitons or the flowing gowns of a Grecian noble; she wears instead dresses of her own design."

"And if the snake should bite?" Leo says.

"She has their fangs removed. Their poison is milked daily. Some are not even poisonous. Who needs guards when one has snakes?"

My box fills: broken items, discarded items, old rope, old fastenings, more sea glass, shells of all kinds, coins, the odd lost ring, a broken chain, feathers, dead butterflies and resin.

We march on. Bedraggled, often hungry, but our feet hardening up and growing another layer of skin that is thicker and more resilient than before. Each night Idahlia and Leo entertain the small group that camps near us. Between us all we find something to cook. Something to drink.

And we are never cold because the good fire burns well. And when we retreat to sleep in our small tent, we lie together using each other as a kind of shield, and as an extra blanket.

Sogdia 331 BC

"Come." Muni says, calling to Roxane, who is taking her time.

The sun shines weak on the stones that pave the way to the forecourt. The three women walk in single file with their heads bowed. Muni leads the small procession, while Roxane follows close behind, Leila is slow up the rear and her feet scuff the rough stones. A lamb bleats and Roxane freezes.

"It's the smallest one." Roxane says.

"He can wait." Muni replies, but Roxane knows full well that the lamb will die before the ceremony is complete.

Leila takes her daughter's hand. Tears spill onto Leila's cheeks; she doesn't bother to wipe the shame of them away.

"I don't want to be betrothed to him." Roxane whispers, placing her words in her mother's ear so that Muni will not hear.

"No, I know, but you must. We are here only to sleep and to labour."

Leila knows well of her daughter's concern. Muni, however, found that her marriage to Oxyartes saved her from a fate more terrible than death itself. Both wives were taken from their homelands at differing times to wed the Baron Oxyartes. The previous wives of Sogdian stock died either in childbirth, along with their child, or from an illness.

Muni comes from the place of solid ice and continual trekking. A place in the north where the wild steppe ponies are tamed. She had shared a tent with all her brothers. The world she knew then was a bitter place, where food was scarce, where one must hold their tongue. Today her task is only to ensure that Roxane comes dressed in the old blue dress of the ancestors and to witness the binding of her son with the beautiful Roxane.

Leila too had come to live in this mountainous rocky outcrop with its fickle winds and deathly cold. The summers like embers on a dull fire, the winters like the bite of a sharp-clawed monster. She had been found rather than fetched. Discovered rather than taken. Traded rather than gifted. In this climate she cuts a lean figure, tall, with long dark hair and brown eyes that look as if they have been cut from amber. Her lashes are long and her skin the colour of honey.

The three women approach the forecourt just as a cloud of sandalwood makes its way to heaven. Oxyartes has his eyes shut and chants. He lifts up his words to their one true Lord above. His beard sways with him and he rocks from side to side.

Roxane takes her place beside her future husband, her half-brother Shapur. She sees her mother's tears; her mother is wrapped in the long brown coat that Muni made her when she arrived, looking just as beautiful as she would have in those silk dresses that hang on the wall of their hut. She sees Muni's smile, as she claps along with the drummers who play the song of the prophet.

Her father, Oxyartes, begins. The old blue dress is itchy and Roxane imagines the tiny creatures that nibble away on its fabric, the same creatures that feast on her mother's silk dresses that hang like faded flowers on the lichen-encrusted walls of their hut. She has the old cloth tucked into the old blue dress's pocket, a piece of stained material that has been used to bind the betrothed together and to catch the drops of nuptial rain.

"We are in Persia but not of it. We follow the laws of our prophet only, not those of satraps, or kings. We live here, keeping what our Lord made and intended for us pure. As my father said and his father before him, a man cannot eat gold."

Oxyartes turns towards his two children. He takes their hands and inspects them before he asks Bah, his younger brother, to bring forth the beer. Shapur, his son, the half-brother of Roxane, drinks first. He is noisy in his thirst. Roxane sips second. And she sips as her mother has taught her. When one eats or drinks, one must take little. One must not be drawn to the act of eating. The food and drink must slip down the throat unnoticed.

"The first kiss, the first binding of these two children of heaven." Oxyartes says, handing Shapur a slab of their own fine bread.

"Now Roxane." He says. She takes the fragrant bread and holds it just for a second to her nose. Then she places her slice to Shapur's slice. Shapur bites. She turns away from his eating. Then she takes but a crumb from the joined bread, places it in her mouth and waits for it to soften.

"The meeting in time of flesh." Oxyartes says. There are songs now. One is sung by Roxane's cousin. This small child, the youngest daughter of Fahr, sings into the flames of their fire which must never be tainted with anything but wood, incense and the cones of the trees.

When she has finished, Oxyartes tosses twelve cones into the flames. Roxane watches as each little segment of the cone becomes lit.

"Twelve sons. We pray for such a miracle, and if a miracle is to happen, we all must be vigilant to the words of our prophet. We must look after what the one true God has given us. This bounty, not to be spoiled by anything."

The women dance, weaving in and out of one another as Oxyartes binds the couple's wrists with the old, stained linen. The men encircle the women.

—

The fire, scented again with sandalwood, emits a large opaque cloud that rises up to meet the face of Mother Moon. The night has come and their Lord has extinguished his one great fire and lit his many lanterns.

Roxane studies the old tree that stands sentinel behind the forecourt. This wise old tree is the protector of their souls while they dwell here on Earth in the balm of their God.

Fahr undoes the pair. He is the son of the mighty Bah, youngest and only surviving brother of Oxyartes. He stalls a little as he unwraps Roxane's wrist. He places his hand on hers for a moment.

He says nothing, but in his eyes she sees a little flicker of anger. He bows his head closer to her. "In heaven, all souls that meet are free."

Roxane thinks of the lamb, free of his earthly home. She heads to the pathway that will take her down to his body. But before she does his bidding, she is stopped by Muni.

"Look up," she says.

A spring snow falls. Light snowflakes that land but melt straight away. Muni collects some in the cupped palm of her hand.

"It is a blessing, Roxane. I know that my son is not so strong. I know that at times he does not see clearly what he should see, nor listen well. His ears are not as they should be. But I do know that when your father brought your mother here all those years ago—that was a blessing, for my husband then had another child. A girl child of good blood, good bones." Muni touches the side of Roxane's head.

Roxane nods and without thinking opens her mouth to receive a snowflake.

"What do they taste of?" Muni says. They often drink melted snow water but it is always boiled and cooled to warm.

Roxane stands still, her feet warm in her soft boots and woollen socks. She stands and says nothing. She is thinking.

"Does it taste of a blessing?"

Roxane does not wish to offend Muni, who has always been kind to her and her mother. She even nursed Roxane as a babe, but Roxane wants to speak only the truth. For that is the way of their Lord, it is what the prophet said so many years ago; that lies are poison, lies place darkness in the world.

Roxane thinks of the roses in her grandfather's garden. Rohan of the Roses is what they call him. He is a satrap in southern Persia. The tales of his garden have become her own story, one that often sends her to sleep when sleep will not come to her. She wants to say the melt tastes of white roses. But she has no idea what they taste like. She thinks that would be a beautiful thing to say, but it would be a lie.

"They taste like stone." She finally says.

"Like stone?" Muni's walnut face screws up towards the moon above. "You eat stones? Would explain how strong you are."

Roxane laughs. "No, but I have sucked on stone when I have been out in the field and very hungry."

"You are a strange one. Where your mother is beautiful, tired and cold all the time, you are warm and you think, Roxane. You think like a lion."

Roxane finds the lamb. He must have put up a good fight for he is still a little warm. She cradles him before taking him to the shed where fresh meat waits to be made good. She knows that he will make a sweet stew and his fleece will be used for the little ones' toes.

She feels her womb and knows that soon she will bleed. She is behind the other girls of her age who already sit in the hut made of sticks and give their blood to the field in need of it most. She listens to the stories when the women return after seven days of rest and nourishment. She knows that this time is the best time for them, even if it begins with an ache. It is where they eat well, drink the green drink for the pain, and converse about how the body is made to please.

Oxyartes' hut is small in comparison to many others. It is hot and stuffy. The elders sit around the old pot-bellied brazier and drink their warm herbal drinks. Roxane sits cross-legged at the rear of the confined room. Shapur sits next to her. His legs move up and down so she puts out her hand to quieten them. If she doesn't do this Oxyartes will start to yell at him.

They listen, as they do each day, as the men discuss the crops, the stock, the horses, the pens that need mending, the rooves that leak.

"You will cut wood this morning," Oxyartes says to his son. Roxane is present because Shapur has difficulty remembering. "And, Roxane, this afternoon you will watch your mother because Sini is not well. Do you understand what you need to do?"

Roxane nods. She has been called upon twice before to guard her mother as she takes her daily stroll to the same outlying field in the south.

"Shapur, this afternoon you will mill grain with your mother." Oxyartes turns his eyes away and talks with Bah, before dismissing the group.

But Shapur moves forward. "He is coming," he yells.

This is not the first time Shapur has said this. It has become something he says to someone most days.

Oxyartes sighs and stands. He calls all his men back and asks them to sit again.

"My son," he says. "We have talked about this before. We are aware of the Macedon's movements. We have spies who look for us. Now I must implore you to cease speaking of this to our people for it makes them frightened, and they have no need to be frightened, for your good uncle here and I have taken care of everything in the event that this man from the west might, and I say *might*, invade us."

This is the same response Roxane's father has given her brother every day since they all learnt of the man called the Macedon, who marches on and on in Persia and captures much land.

"Roxane, can you help him hold his tongue?"

She cannot. That would be a lie, but she can comfort him when he grows agitated and tell him that her father would not lie about the precautions he and Bah have taken to protect them.

It is unseasonably cold. The harvest has come and gone. Sometimes in the last moments of the season of bounty, it is magnificent in Sogdia. She remembers golden light on the surrounding hills, a warm kind of southern breeze that smells so different to the normal chilling one. But this season, the Greeks' advancement seems to have made the air solemn and rigid. She lies on the hard stalks of this year's barley. It was a good year for the crop. She knows that the stalks will make indents on her stomach.

Her mother turns around, counting out her steps. She wears her brown woollen coat; its fur cuffs have become matted. Her hood is up and the fur that lines it is wispy and moulting. Her hands reach deep into her pockets. She faces the south mainly, watching, looking, regarding. Then the west, then the east. In each spot she removes her hood to see better. When she faces north she bows her head and mourns something. It is a sad picture, and every time she witnesses it Roxane feels something sharp sting her inside.

Leila moves back, her feet light on the crisp earth, which is frosting up already. Roxane takes her time to rise, feeling that this act of spying is unnecessary, and she does not want her mother to know that she has been directed to this task today. As she opens her eyes fully to the landscape around her, she sees three birds of prey circling on the far eastern border. *Some beast is dying or dead.* There are banks of dense black clouds on the horizon.

She runs to the stables. "Fahr, something for us in the east."

Fahr looks up from his post and frowns. "No, you are not to." But Roxane already has a harness on Minoo. She leaps up from a small step and places her feet either side of the mare's girth.

Fahr grabs the reins. "No, Roxane, there is a storm coming." He pulls the reins back and she fights for control of them.

"Good meat. It is ours," she says.

Fahr shakes his head. He looks around at his lot, at his own little empire as he calls it. He is the head stableman and he loves each and every animal. He often speaks to her about their breeding. How the Arab stallions make the most beautiful horses; the most beautiful in all the world. And now her father has not only the most beautiful herd but the strongest too, for he and his father, Bah, put these fine stallions to the short stubby steppe ponies of the north. Strength and power, beauty and grace.

Fahr relents. "All right, I will ride with you."

They reach the outcrop of rocks and scrub. It is a lot further than she imagined. Fahr dismounts first, holding her back with his hand. The birds screech overhead. They fly a little higher, but they do not leave their prey.

"It's a man." Fahr calls back to her. She slips her mount, tethers Minoo to a thin, reedy tree and creeps over to the body. She bows down and listens to his chest. Then she licks her finger and places it close to his lips. "He is alive." she says.

Together they lift the man and Fahr places him on Hosh, a thickset Arabian with a snort like a horn. Hosh tosses his head to and fro and allows Fahr to secure the man to the front of his rump. Then Fahr leaps up and sits behind the old man, holding him into his chest. Roxane has placed her own cape out for Fahr to wrap him in, but he protests: "Roxane, it is cold."

All the tribe lines the steps of the incline to see their return. Roxane feels her stomach bite her as she thinks about her father's wrath towards her.

Fahr pats her leg as they walk up to the forecourt. "It was my idea and I didn't know you were following," he says.

"He knows me and knows me well," Roxane replies. "He won't like a lie."

As the weather is sharp, the fire on the forecourt has been lit. Oxyartes places the sandalwood in its orange belly and lifts up his arms and his eyes to the great God above.

Oxyartes makes everyone wait; his silence is like a stone that can't be moved. The cool air finds its way into even the warmest toes so the tribe has moved closer together, nearer to the fire and their eyes study the foreigner. Muni tends to the man, with her firm and strong arms she tucks three woollen blankets around his inert body and lays his head upon a bolster. Oyxartes clears his throat.

"Well, what do you think, Roxane?" Oxyartes bellows at her.

"Possibly a spy, father, of the Macedonians."

"And you, Fahr, what do you add to this, or take away from this, or assume?"

"Wise uncle, I do believe he is Greek."

"What tells you this?"

"His complexion is quite fair. He made a few words in his unconscious state. He spoke of the Great Herodotus."

"Yes, Herodotus," Roxane says.

"Oh, he did, did he? Well then, I say it is good you have captured him. He now becomes trade. And he becomes a person who holds information. It will be valuable."

"If he lives," Muni says. "Oxyartes—he's weak."

"What man goes out in a storm such as this?" Bah says. But as soon as he has said it, he encounters the raised brows of his brother whose gaze is now upon his own son and the beautiful Roxane.

Roxane speaks as the crowd remain stunned. Silent. "I think perhaps he's not with the army of the Macedon, for the clothes he wears are not those of a warrior."

"Spies by their very definition disguise themselves," Oxyartes says.

"But he does not wear dark clothes that would merge into the land. He wears the colourful robes of a man who lives in the east."

Oxyartes motions with his hand for Muni to unwrap the imposter. And under the jacket that Roxane put upon him is a bright, long top, flecked with crimson-and-gold, and a colourful scarf. Under this are breeches made of snakeskin. He wears soft boots, like their own, not the hard sandals worn by the Greeks. She has listened to the elders talk of the Macedons; their specific attire of leather, metal plates, sandals made of hard leather, helmets of silver. He wears no dark cape. His head is quite bare but for his silver hair, which is thinning. There are copper bangles on his wrists, and he wears a necklace of some kind. She bends down for a closer look. It is in the shape of an elephant. She knows these creatures from her mother's tales. The elephants, the bright-coloured birds, the exotics from the east. How her grandfather had some animals like this in his compound.

Her father sends the crowd away but tells Fahr, Bah, Muni and Roxane to stay. He squats down and replaces the warmth given to this man. He doesn't say anything for a long time. "Muni, make him live. Do whatever you can to bring him to life."

Muni nods, and already on her fingers she is counting out and remembering her potions, her salves, murmuring these for all of us to hear. The wormwood, the drink of green which brings fire to the belly and clarity to the mind; honey, the best of it; warm water boiled with mint. Pastes of meat and apricots soaked in the milk of the young calf.

Oxyartes turns to his daughter and his stableman. "Take turns to watch him. Fahr, take him to the hut of my wives and daughter. Lay him beside the brazier, turn him so that each side of him becomes warm. Remember anything that he might say, for in this state of sleep the body lets out the secrets of the mind."

He taps Roxane on her shoulder. "I think you are right. This is no soldier. A spy you would expect to

employ the tactics of the well-trained arm of the military.
This man risked a storm; he did not read the winds. His
nails have been plucking through undergrowth. His feet
are blistered; they are not the hardened feet of a warrior
or warlord. He has not been fed. He has not learnt to
forage off the land to keep himself alert."

Once the man, Phaidros, recovers, Roxane and Shapur sit
in his hut. He has told them all that he is no more a spy
than he is bird. He has spent much time in conversation
with Oxyartes telling him about his travels; how he felt
the calling of the world, how he wanted to follow in the
footsteps of the great Herodotus. That he had been raised
in Ithaca, the youngest of many children and that when
his dear mother died he took his cloak and walked, then
sailed in small boats. Then walked again.

"India, it's a blessing, children," he says,
describing that wonderful land so full of colour; so full of
the most delicious foods and fragrance, and interesting
people. "Yes, I longed to stay there," he says, "but my
heart pulled me back west. To the sea. I want to die on the
shore, at Troy. Where the great Achilles and his lover
Patroclus died."

It is like this most days. Roxane and Shapur walk
to the Greek's hut just as the dew starts to dry. They sit in
the hut which he has spent much time decorating with
foliage and fresh flowers, candles and old disused
wooden furniture. They are here to be taught the language
of the invader, for Phaidros has persuaded their father that
words are more powerful than any weapon. That if one
person in his tribe could talk to the cheeky Macedonian,
as he calls him, then that could mean a better deal for
them. Alexander respects such things, as his father did
before him.

And Phaidros is testimony, is he not? For he speaks three or four tongues and this has stood him in very good stead. The locals love him everywhere he goes.

Roxane enjoys the sessions, Shapur not so much. He finds the lessons hard. He cannot recite the words like she can. But Phaidros does not worry so much and says that she will be able to talk for him.

The days are drawing in. The great cold is upon them. Phaidros stokes his brazier and takes the black beer warm.

Shapur fills his cup but Roxane does not. She takes only the warmed water in the copper basin on his stove top. She pulls her wrap around her and sits so that she can rub the tips of her boots, should she get cold.

"Tell me, what do you know of the world?" Phaidros says this morning.

It is never the same, the day of learning. One day he makes them learn a poem, the next he stands and acts out the great feats of the Trojan War. Another day he arranges a series of implements on his small table: a spoon, a trowel, a cup, a bowl, a blanket, and he will make them say their names in Greek, until their tongues feel as if they will fall out of their mouths.

But this day, it is this question.

Shapur is mute. His face pales.

Roxane stands and walks towards the flames. "We live in this area, secluded. I know only of the world through my mother's tales. Muni, Shapur's mother, does not really speak of the world she came from because she says it was too bleak. Too hard. But my mother came from a world far away."

"But what have you experienced of the world, dear Roxane?"

She cannot think of anything to say so she just places some words out into the room, to fill it. "Shells on the ground and stars in the sky."

"Explain."

She twists her fingers and rises on her toes. She inhales. She thinks of the shells that her mother keeps in their hut. Seashells she gathered on the sands of an ocean. Leila told Roxane that long ago her father had taken her and her sisters to see the blue. That her sisters had threaded the shells through her hair. "The colour of white is the colour of the shells and the stars, the little lanterns of our God are white too," Roxane says

"Go on."

She pauses. Sits down on the funny little bench that Phaidros has cobbled together and places the colourful silk scarf that he wore on arrival over her knees. "In between them is rich soil. The soil is made even richer by green growth and our golden crops."

"Yes, very good. Let me expand. The spirals of a shell; the shell is a home for a creature to live in. The creature is part of the ocean. Hard outer shell, soft creature inside." Phaidros rubs the bristles of his beard. "Stars are bright, sparkling heavens, sparkling shells. There may be a connection. Yes, not necessarily a whole world view but good thoughts. Thank you my dear."

When they arrive the next day, Phaidros places a snail shell upon his table. "I could not find any shells this far inland, but I did find this on my walk yesterday."

Roxane turns the shell over and examines it.

"What do you see?"

"It is brown striped on the outside and pale blue on the inside."

"What do you say to this?"

Roxane rolls over on the outer sides of her boots and then the sides of her feet roll in again. Shapur sits on a small stool not far from her and stares into space.

"The kill," she says.

"The kill?"

"Yes, the hunt. When we hunt a deer—the outside of her skin is brown and sometimes striped. Her innards are blue."

Phaidros smiles at her and then taps the top of her head with his long, ringed fingers. "I will have you speaking like a Greek Elite in no time. You are doing well, Roxane, your mind is sharp. You are observant. You listen well. You talk well. Now it is time to learn how to speak like a noble."

Roxane lifts the snail's shell to her ear. "There is no sound of the sea in here," she says.

Phaidros turns to look at her. He looks at all of her. "No, the snail that once lived in this shell was not a creature of the sea."

Phaidros dismisses her but he keeps Shapur. He tells her that from now on she will need to tune her mind. The lessons will be hard. And after the lessons are done she must repeat all that they have learnt that day as she goes about her tasks, and as she falls asleep at night.

The welcome warm weather arrives after many moons of the cold. Roxane is thankful for this time with Phaidros. She has grown to love this life of learning. She walks ahead of her brother and imagines that soon, the scorching heat will be upon them. She doesn't mind the hot, hot, time but for some in her tribe it is testing and she wonders how she could make it more pleasant for them.

Shapur is behind her, dawdling, and when she approaches the hut, the door is closed.

The air is still and she senses something. She knocks on the door. Quietly at first then loudly.

Perhaps he has gone walking, but this is not usual at this time of day. She waits some more before lifting the latch so that the door opens. The air inside is foul. She smells it immediately. The poison weed.

She runs to Phaidros who is prone on the floor, his lips caked in dried spittle, vomit on the floor beside him. She lifts his cup. It is empty. The scent of death.

Shapur rushes to the old man's side. He cries, sobs. "Wake up, wake up."

Roxane feels pity, sorrow. She places her arm around her brother, but he shakes her off. He starts to slap the dead man's face. "Wake up, wake up!"

Roxane runs outside. Muni and Oxyartes are already there. "It's for the best," Muni says. Roxane is too shocked to speak.

"You are well schooled now," Oxyartes says. "Phaidros was so proud of what he had achieved. He said your accent is Athenian, that you speak with the grace of a goddess. That all the words are now in your heart."

"And Shapur?" Roxane says.

Muni shrugs.

Her father walks away.

That afternoon, as is their custom, they take the body of Phaidros to the hill on the northern side. A quiet open place where the birds will come for him. Shapur stands beside her. His grief is unbearable. Her father chants to the God overhead. The death chant. A chant that urges the last release of lies so that the soul can fly up to the silver bridge of judgement. That hopes the man will not be tempted by the evil ones but set free to live in the great golden kingdom beyond.

Her father does not linger and leads his people back down to their homelands. Roxane stays, with Shapur.

"I will see him again, won't I?" Shapur says.

Roxane remains silent, for to tell him so would be a lie. She knows that the great birds of prey will not touch this body for they will smell the poison too.

"He wanted to take me with him. As soon as you were convers … convers … We were going to go to the sea." Shapur breaks down again and kneels in the long, dry, sticky grass.

Roxane sees Muni in the distance. She approaches.

"Roxane, leave him. I will see to him now."

Persepolis 330 BC

I check the wind. The tail of smoke flares out to the east. The fire will not turn towards us unless the wind changes direction.

I tell this to Old Leo, who not a moment ago was fumbling with the lacing that makes our tent secure. The old man's hands are knobbly and red, and I heard him yell out.

"Fire, be quick about it."

The three of us are standing in the civilian camp with many others. We watch as the Palace of Persepolis burns.

We drink wine under our awning with the lamps lit around us. The civilians speak of their fear. But I shout out to them that for now we are spared.

"Thank the Gods, that you insisted we bring the washing in each night, my love," Idahlia says. It is hot and the sweat rains down her face. Leo pours himself more wine.

I do not trust a night to laundry. The weather can change, and if this smoke did come to us then we would need to rewash everything. It's funny but I have come to like this new occupation of ours. I stand guard like a soldier, shooing away the enemy: small birds, thieves, and my wife's hands. Her impatience to get her work done often means she takes it in damp. But it is no good, laundry that is not yet dry goes musty, smells.

I have constructed lines between two branches of fallen wood. And if we are in transit, I simply string rope out, placing the wood firm into the sides of our carts. The movement gives adequate breeze and assists with the drying.

It's Idahlia that rises early to collect the day's catch. Well, that is what I call it. The morning's catch, the evening's harvest. She converses and gossips with the soldiers, the generals' manservants, the courtesans and any other person willing to part with some kind of payment in exchange for laundry well done.

That afternoon I walk to the palace to inspect the damage. The Syrian seer, who has caught Alexander's attention on more than one occasion, for her predictions do tend to come true, is dancing about on the fringe of the fire. With her staff in one hand, she chants in a language foreign to me. She tosses small stones onto the cindered land to her right.

She turns one eye towards me, the other stays with the small flames that lick the ground. "He does not like this. This fire has destroyed the pearl. Alexander is innocent of this flame. It is her with her fishy birth that did hurl the flare into the hall." She stops and spits. Then she counts the stones in her hands. "Five stones, one, two, three, four, five."

She hobbles over to me. She is a dark-cloaked women who smells of faeces and urine. "See." She holds the stones out to me in her craggy palm. "See!"

I shake my head.

"Five families, five more layers before the last one is killed by a serpent. By her own hand," she says.

"Do you speak of Alexander?"

"No, you fool, of the fisherman's daughter, from Athens. Thais." She spits out her name.

I'm not following her words. I'm tired from our night's vigil. I walk away but she catches my arm with her nails. "You will see it, Andronicus, you will witness this atrocity." Her eyes cloud over and she is suddenly crippled with fatigue. She stumbles and falls. I try to pick her up but she waves me away. "She is the one who ruined this beauty. This palace. Ruination. Fish caught, filleted. Scales on her eyes. She is the one …"

Fida, the Syrian Seer gasps and then screams, and then she cowers away like a cornered animal.

A soldier has listened to her. "It's true, the courtesan Thais was dancing in the great hall with the General Ptolemy and many other besides them. It was she who led the dance in honour of Dionysus. It was she who threw a flare into the hay under the main table. I saw it with my own eyes."

I nod.

"They say Alexander, whose wing was spared by the way, is not so happy about this. But many are. I mean, what better way to say to the Persians, to the cowardly King Darius, that we have taken the most revered palace of them all?"

I linger, for fire is a fascinating subject. Her ways, her movements, the heat, the noise, even. Many hoplites are thrashing wet cloths among the stubborn tongues of flame that are persistent, insistent that they live.

The crowd is large but I have found a small nook, shelter under a tree that is not singed. It's not long before others join me. Beside me stands a stranger, of tall build, and dark hair. He wears clothes of soft leather. His odour is good. He has tethered a fine steed to the trunk of this lonely tree. And as I squat down, he does too.

"The palace was fine," he says. His speech is accented but he articulates our tongue well.

"Yes, I believe it was."

"Fine friezes and stone workings. A fine hall where traders from all corners of the world would meet to barter, collect coin, trade, and converse. It was a place of wonder and sharing."

This man has deep green eyes and I like him without knowing why.

"Are you hungry?"

The stranger replies that he could eat a horse. He looks over to his beautiful mare. "But not that one."

Zek sits on the rug we salvaged from the bloodied battlefield of Gaugamela. The deer and birds in its weave play among the dark green and gold forest. I spent days cleaning it, bringing it back to life. The folded clean laundry sits around us like small cloth towers.

"Where are you from?" Idahlia asks.

"Well …" He stalls. Then he continues, "I am from nowhere in particular."

"But you must have been born somewhere," she says.

"Oh yes, I was born into a family that moved about from place to place in order to find enough grazing for our herd."

"And do you do that now?"

"No." He stops and drinks some wine. "This is very good wine, Andronicus."

"Yes, with our work now we trade whatever we can to make our life more pleasant."

"And that is how it should be," Zek says.

"Tell me about your family then," Idahlia says.

"My mother died when I was young. My father had too many mouths to feed so I left to mine silver."

"So that is what you do?"

"No, not now."

I serve up a platter of goats' cheese, some olives, some flat bread.

"So thankful for this, Andronicus, and Idahlia, thank you very much. Your hospitality is splendid, splendid."

He is well spoken, this traveller. I look at his hands for clues as to his occupation; they are not rough.

He sees me looking at them. "Oils, precious oils, used for any kind of old leathery skin like mine, even my horse likes me to rub them on her. These leather clothes …" He plucks up a sample of his elegant clothing. "Even this leather, I believe, is subject to wax and oils and some other secret ingredient. They tell me it is … chewed."

"We use spit and urine. To bring out the whites, don't we Andronicus?"

I nod. "And who has to collect the piss pots?" I place my finger on my chest.

"So tell us what is in your travel bags." Like his clothes, the travel bags are of fine leather.

Zek stands and stretches out his limbs. "It's the most beautiful thing of all."

"You are not going yet? I mean we have hardly got to know you?" Idahlia says.

"I must contemplate what I do next. You see, I have lost my market here."

I pour him some more wine and tell him to sit. If he wants to spend the night under in our tent he is most welcome. He refuses the offer but takes more wine, sipping it and savouring each mouthful. He takes another piece of bread.

"Have you come from the east?" I ask him.

Zek smiles. "What gave it away?"

"The jade."

Zek fingers the pendant that hangs off a gold chain around his neck. He takes from his pocket a string of lighter green beads "For you, for your kindness."

I examine them. They are exquisite.

"So you carry this green upon you?" Idahlia says.

"No. I carry silk."

Idahlia is silent. Silk. Fabric.

"Tell us from where it comes?" I say.

He crosses his legs. "From the most beautiful land. I walk across these lands to the east, then I take a guide and a small boat and we journey by sea to the place of the deepest greens you have ever seen. It is here that I stop and trade gold with the local people.

He stops to look at us both. "It is really quite sublime. And quite an odd feat of the world in which we live, for you see the creature that makes the silk expels it from their nether regions. Like the silk of a spider but it is much finer. This thread is then spun, and it is woven into great cloth. Then the maidens of this place dye the cloth using their secret mixes. The cloth then hangs in ancient trees and dries by the light of the moon."

"Andronicus doesn't let anything dry by the light of the moon. And I can tell you a fairytale too, Zek. You see, I work with silk. I once dressed the mother of our King. Alexander's mother, yes, I dressed her. Sewed up fine garments, some of silk."

Zek's eyes have gone faraway. He is making his way up to farewell us.

"Can we buy your silk?" Idahlia says.

Zek shakes his head. "No, I will need my silk to stock the change I need to make."

"Where will you go?" I ask.

"I have been thinking about this for some time, Andronicus, and as the world has whispered to me now in the wake of this fire. It's time to change."

"We have wealth to pay you for your wares," Idahlia says, and she walks to the back of our tent, to the screen behind and I can hear her as she digs up the grass tile. Under the tile the box lies.

———

49

I try to prevent my wife from engaging any further. I know her and I know she makes at times impetuous decisions. So I gather up Zek and his things and lead him to the tent doorway. "So where will you go?" I say, seeing his patient horse outside, her tail flicking away the menacing flies.

"To Samarkand. It's a glorious place. I will set up shop there, sell the silk from a stationary place. This is the way, isn't it. When one moves, one's feet grow weary and yearn for a shelter that will not blow away."

"Or burn," I say.

Idahlia has circumvented us and is standing by the horse. She pleads with us to go back inside. "We must show Zek our things, for we can I'm sure persuade him that if the silk is left for us, we will do great things with it."

My brow beads a fine nervous sweat. There is no market for new clothes here, for the reinforcements carry new uniforms with them. They deliver fresh chitons not only from Greece, but also from the linen weavers of Egypt. And then there is the blatant 'borrowing', from the locals who might sport a fine article upon them. Many of the elite dress in the exotic clothes of these regions.

Idahlia proceeds. The Fates do not stop her. Zek kneels down and inspects the items she places on the rug. He runs his fingers through the retrieved and now cleaned lost rings, necklaces, loose stones. He moves his nails slowly over each item, placing a few by his side.

He rises, and loosens one of his saddle bags. He pulls out a bundle of orange and then a bundle of pink.

Idahlia meets his gaze. She places more in front of him. Piles up the silver as if she was a moneylender. "Idahlia, I am so sorry, but you see silver is plentiful for me. When I am in a state of flux, I mine it, craft it into small things. Another way to survive."

This does not deter my wife; she is now placing the sea glass, the resin, an animal's tooth that I have carved into the shape of a fish, the old copper pot that my mother passed back to me, filled with her tears.

Zek smiles. He places all the sea glass in a pile. "It is delightful, isn't it, this jewel given up by sea. Lost, rough and sharp, made smooth by the sand, water and salt." He turns to me. "I think they would make a nice addition to my selling counter. Imagine them in a clear glass vase."

Zek takes blues and greens from his bag and lays them on the carpet. He takes up the miniature copper pot and turns it in his fingers. "Don't you love miniature things?" He smiles. But he does not take the tooth fish, nor the resin. He begins to move again.

"Do you have whites, creams?"

"Yes, they are the most valuable of all."

Idahlia then takes our gold. My father's gift.

Zek looks hesitant.

"I want it all." Idahlia says.

Zek unpacks his bag, laying out the remaining material he has, rubbing his chin. Thinking all the time. He places the traded items in his bag, leaving the gold till last.

"Are you sure, Andronicus? About the gold, I mean."

I cannot speak. I do not have any words. I nod; my head moves without my noticing it move.

Zek brushes down his trousers once more. "That is that then. I will not be heading north to Sarmarkand, but east. To the lands that some say are the paradise that all people dream about."

I walk out with him, shading my eyes as the bright sun of Persepolis hits me. The smoke has dissipated. The

---

people have gone back to their dwellings. The horse snorts upon seeing her master. Zek leaps up onto his back. "She will enjoy this. Her load is a little lighter."

Just as he starts to turn her head using the bit and leather strappings, he leans over towards me. He takes something from his pocket and lays it flat in the palm of my hand.

"For you, Andronicus. A good luck charm. A talisman, I believe the Greeks call it."

I look at it, puzzled, and before I can thank him he has turned and gone.

In my palm the face of a five-pointed star looks at me. It is etched. I see a mountain peak, a river, some ripples which must represent the sea. A valley, a tree. And in the sky above, three gems. Little crude gems. It is not a piece that one would describe as delicate. He must have made it himself. Perhaps in those long evenings when he would have camped out under the stars. It is silver and I turn it over to discover on the other side a highly polished void. Just plain silver, shining in this sun.

I sit down and play with it for a bit before placing it in my pocket. I will need good luck, for even if we wanted to turn for home, even if we wanted to hire a guide, we could not. The gold is gone. Choice is gone. How quick one's life changes. Zek is heading back to the silk. We are heading north to pursue the runaway King and to forge these outer lands to the ones we already have.

The Sogdian Rock 327 BC

What we would have given for the arid heat of Persepolis, or the rough coastal paths, as this northern bitter wind rages and wages war upon us. We struggle to find any tiny bit of comfort beneath the Sogdian Rock. What I would give to have had that gold again; the gold that lay under the gaze of the Fates. Gold to take us far away from this cold. Cold like a beast, cold that turns flesh blue and gashes the lungs.

Idahlia curls her body into mine, threading it through so that she may gain just one slither of warmth. She is ill with the cold.

Our tent is threadbare. And of course we do not launder, for each and every one of us keeps upon their person any little vestige of clothing.

The cold has spawned a mould; it clothes the interior of the tent that was once new. Fresh from the tanner in Pella. Now it is nothing more than a worn-out coat of some animal.

Boreas, the god of the stinging north wind, howls like some wild monster. A vengeful wind tries to uproot us from the ice that cakes the ground. We are at the edge of Tartarus.

Leo lives. Like Idahlia, he lies inside his wretched tent. His long hair runs down his withered back in knots, and he has wrapped his feet in scraps of cloth.

I keep a fire going. Many struggle to it and try to thaw themselves in front of its flames. I steal wood from the fringes of the military camp and pick up any kindling that I see set into the solid land.

I hear Leo shout out in the night. "The fool. Alexander. What King? What is worse than a fool?" I wait and Leo shouts the answer. "A stubborn fool!"

And then it comes, the second verse, said over and over again not long ago as he sat around this very fire. His voice is deep and melodious. "What is worse, yes what is worse than a stubborn fool?"

"A stubborn stupid fool." I say to the few bodies that lie around. I finish the ode that Leo has created on this Sogdian soil.

I poke at the flames, place more firewood upon them. The wood is dry; good wood chopped by the hoplites, set to dry under the eaves of great trees that surround the military encampment. This wood does not feed us, but it does provide us with a means to melt the ice and snow that is at hand. We drink with our hands firmly around the bowls of our cups.

Aman who I do not know speaks to us as though we are his children. "Alexander waits for this savage Baron. He who has camped high upon this rock that shadows us. Three sheer sides of rock. One treacherous route up to his lair, guarded by his men who lie hidden behind rocks with poison arrows."

The man is breathless, but he continues. "There is no way to reach this man. He is the head of a small tribe that threatens no one. Why not pass him by, leave him on his rock? He has little, this Baron Oxyartes, no gold, no fortune. Why not pass him by?"

"They say he has horses. A breed that would be at home in the stables of the Gods." I say.

"Well if he does have horses up there, I would say they will all be dead by now. This cold kills even the strongest of us."

I take the pot of melted snow from the rod of metal that is suspended over the flame. I have put some stones in the water and some small grubs that I found while digging in the rough grass. With a spoon I take out them out and mash them between my fingers, place them on the back of a spoon and take them to my Idahlia. I feed her like a mother bird feeds her chicks.

The following day Leo is quiet. I make my way to his tent. His body is stiff and my knees go weak. I fall down and touch his cold skin. I roll his body over, his eyes are glazed like days old fish. I have no strength to bury him.

That night I take my box and close my eyes. There is no rattle within it for we have used up all our silver in trade for food. But it does contain some of the silk. Idahlia wrapped it so carefully in linen. In the seams of those wrappings she placed dried herbs to stop the mites from biting. She used wax to seal the edges and some fine cured hide to overwrap it all. The rest is stored in a bag of leather which she purchased from the tanner in Persepolis before we left. Sachets of herbs sweeten its sides, and salt packets soak up the damp.

I dare not look inside the box but I stroke the faces of the Fates. From their mother's blue cloak they fell to earth. When they landed, small fires played upon the earth. Nyx, their mother, cried and her tears extinguished the flames. I stroke the hair of Clotho. I made her hair thicker than the others', for it is she that spins the thread of life. A life that is given to us all. I cry. My tears fall on the wood and make spots like rain. I touch Lachesis, the one who decides if our thread is short or long; she is the one who measures. Then I stroke Atropos. I have carved a tiny pair of scissors into her small hand. Her hair is tight in a knot on top of her head. She is the one who cut the thread.

I look over to Idahlia. She will be next to go. Atropos will cut the golden thread of her life, just as she did old Leo's.

I only go out to put more wood on the fire, to keep those who decide to stay by my flame warm.

When I wake the next day I have a dream in me, memories of a grand time. A time I have not lived yet but which seemed so real. My father is there; he is young and jovial and he is urging me to take the silver. To make my fire roar and . He is laughing. *Go, go. Turn that fire into an inferno my son.* He is clad in his leather apron, and I can hear his hammer upon his anvil. I hear him hum the fine tunes of his own father. *You see they lie there for you. Inside their form are more forms waiting to be found. Like seven silver fishes swimming in the sea. Beside the body of the one who kept light in your camp, whose words filled your heart when you could no longer speak for the fatigue had set tight within you. The body holds these in wait for you. The same body who made your Idahlia blossom. The one who convinced your wife to step outside and bask in a new glory. You owe it to her my son. To your wife*

I rise and I can see my father hovering in the mist outside. *Beckoning me forth . Now do for her what she has done for you . My scepticism is long gone . For you have gone and I must stand with you tonight and many nights to come until the seven silver fish swim. I see your heart for what it is. A separate beautiful soul.*

I feel heat. One man has fed my fire all night and it blazes like Apollo's shield. I walk, not knowing what I am doing or where I am going, but my feet take me to the tomb, the tent of my dear friend Leo.

I rifle through his bags. He was a collector, a thief. He stole to stay alive. He stole words from other people when he knew that they would make another laugh. He told stories that lifted up the weariest of our neighbours and those further afield. He humoured Idahlia when she thought she was not worthy. He lifted her up.

Leo invented the term eavesdropping. Hiding in whatever eave he could and listening in. We came to know much from this activity, but his intention was never really to gather information, it was to curate stories; stories that shocked, stories that made us laugh.

I find silver platters in his bags; I find silver cups. I find one silver hair ornament; I find three rings.

That night I light more fire. I take my tools and a stool, and I cover my legs with Leo's old tent. It is strange, but no persons come this night to keep me company around the fire. To drink in the warmth of snow melt. To chew on a blade of bitter sharp grass. To suck on a stone or a toasted grub. There is no one but me, the full moon above, my fiery pit and my assembled forge.

Upon the Sogdian Rock 327 BC

Roxane dips the silver cup into the slow filtering stream that runs through the back of their cave. The water is pale blue in colour and flickers with the light from the many candles that Muni has placed in all the stone nooks.

They hide here, but the invader camps below.

"He cannot get to us," Oxyartes reassures them every day as they meet on the forecourt to receive their rations and to hear about any other precautions they should take.

She thinks this, knows how well protected they are but still, deep down in her toes, she feels something; a restlessness.

Roxane watches Muni and her mother sleep. They sleep often and enjoy this break from the fields, from the cook house, from the place where they wash clothing and bedding in large wooden barrels.

Their brazier is warm, the cave is warm. The stone which holds them has heated up.

She practises her Greek. She makes sure she dances inside to the tunes in her head. For she knows a body as much as a mind must be kept nimble. She has watched Muni fatten and become breathless. Her mother the opposite.

The food is cold, always. Salted or steeped in oil, fat or honey. There are nuts at every meal, beer, and dried plums. The boiled snow and ice water fizzes in the pot on the brazier.

All is well, she thinks. She must think this.

"Oh, he will grow tired, this Macedon. He will realise that we have nothing special to give him. He will pass us by." Her father says this to them every day.

Another day on the rock. Oxyartes' face is not the same as it was yesterday. There is a crease on his forehead and he has grown pale. He twists his beard. "There was a messenger," he tells them all.

The boys at the side continue to fill the baskets and wooden boxes with food.

"He spoke our tongue well, dressed in fancy Persian clothes. He asked that we might receive a delegation from the King of the Conquered World."

The silence hovers just like the clouds hover. There is no wind today to blow the grey away.

"So we have consented. Only Bah, Shapur, Fahr and I will receive them. We will do so in one of the lower caves so these men of questionable intent do not set foot upon the sacred peak of our home in the sky."

As Roxane prepares to carry one of their baskets and return to the cave of stream and pale white stone, she is pulled to one side by Fahr. "Come," he says.

He takes her hand and leads her to a cave set higher than those below, one she has never set foot in. But when she enters she smells her father's old odour. She smells the beer. His old pot-bellied brazier sits there—it is older than her father and in need of some repair.

"Sit," Oxyartes tells her.

Roxane sits by his mussed-up bed. She sees a shell beside the cushions at the end of it. Her mother has been here.

Fahr stays at the entrance. He is blocking the thin sun that is trying to pierce the clouds. She wishes he would move for she would like to feel the heat on her back.

"Roxane. You hear Greek, you understand it. Therefore tomorrow when these four foreigners come as our guests, you will hide yourself behind a large basket that will sit in a corner of the cave we have chosen to host the meeting in."

She nods.

"At the end of the talks you are to confirm what they have said. You must remember all the words, so that you can tell me later if we missed anything vital."

She whispers a yes, bows her head and places her hands together; she rests her chin on the tips of her fingers. He has not yet dismissed her.

"One more task for you," her father says. "If you see anything untoward—a hand going into a pocket secretly, a drawing from a garment of some substance, a noise from outside that is not of our making …"

She waits. The cold is almost unbearable. The stone in this cave is wet and dark and grey, the floor dusted with leaves. "Then, my dear, you will tip over the basket in front of you. The basket will be filled with oranges.

"Yes, Father."

"Now repeat back to me what you are to do tomorrow."

The cave they have chosen has been made welcoming. The brazier is Bah's. It is fine, tall and highly polished, and its light is soft. The best carpets and furs have been laid around the cave's interior. Roxane finds the basket. It is tall and of fine weave and inside are the fragrant oranges eaten only on special occasions. She places herself behind it.

As if hunting, she takes note of the setting. She closes her eyes and waits. Her heart beats too hard and she breathes deep and low, stilling the beat until it no longer deafens her. She waits while the men meet the delegation outside and then she hears the thuds; the sound of feet walking on the stone.

The steps grow closer and closer.

She sees them enter.

Three tall men. One shorter. The shorter one speaks in their tongue. He wears a great cloak with embroidered suns on its back.

He speaks well and slowly and she hears him introduce the strangers.

"General Ptolemy. Faithful servant of our leader. General Hephaestion. General Craterus. And you already met me, on the day I walked up to your fine station here to ask that we meet. I'm Peucestas, General Peucestas, and we are very grateful Baron Oxyartes for the opportunity to talk to you. We have brought gifts."

Roxane sees this man of fine clothes place a bag down to the right of the circle.

Her father, Bah, Fahr and Shapur all ignore the bag. Her father does not reciprocate with a formal introduction; instead he tells them all to sit. He clicks his fingers and Fahr pours the beer.

They all drink. Fahr offers them the best of their preserved fruits and flat bread.

No one speaks. Roxane observes the attire of the three other guests. The Generals. They wear what she considers traditional Greek military uniform, the very same description that Phaidros gave her of the fine soldiers of the west. Leather, fittings in dull metal. She sees on their calves big knives slid into leather scabbards. She watches their hands.

General Ptolemy plays with his hands, holding them together, unlatching them, refolding them. General

Hephaestion has his arms folded. General Craterus has his hands on the rug by his side; he leans slightly back. He has long fair hair and a skin tanned under the great lamp of their lord.

"What is it you wish to talk to us about?" her father says.

Peucestas translates and then points to General Ptolemy.

The General stands. But her father puts out his hand and lowers it several times, so the General known as Ptolemy sits.

"We ask that you might surrender. This is not a heinous thing to do; rather it is a noble thing to do. For in doing so you will advance your people. Your boys will receive an education. They will then go on to be recruited into the fine academies and military training schools. We can assure you they will become the best fighters, the best sailors even, the best the world has ever known. In surrendering, you, Baron, will be made the satrap of Sogdia. These are our terms. They are generous."

She listens as the translator as Peucestas repeats the terms. He does so well. There is nothing inaccurate in his translation.

Oxyartes waits. Ptolemy plays again with his fingers. Hephaestion yawns. Craterus seems almost to smile but not in a rude way. It is as if he is impressed by Oxyartes.

"If I may add?" Ptolemy begins.

Oxyartes nods after Peucestas translates.

"We know of the northern ways of combat, and Alexander finds them intriguing. Impressive, even. We would like you to know that we can learn from you too. Your input would be valuable."

When her father speaks, he says only, "What would those be. Our ways?"

Peucestas poses the question to Ptolemy.

"Well … subterfuge, surprise attacks, and we know you are expert horsemen and hunters."

Fahr pours more beer while Peucestas intercedes with words that differ only in that he puts them to her father in a more desirable way. "We are strangers to a warfare played in secret. We have always preferred to battle on an open plain, in full view of our enemy, who also plays this way. But we are interested to learn about your ways, Baron Oxyartes. Alexander admires the way you carry out not only your business but also how you protect your people."

The General Hephaestion drains his cup. He takes two slices of flat bread and a handful of dried peaches.

"Well, we have nothing of value for you," her father says. "We hold no gold, no gems, no spices, nothing that the trading hall of our now dead Darius would receive. We crop, we feed our people, we are careful not to taint the waters with skin or waste. We feed our soil so that the crops will nourish our blood and bones. We answer only to our one true God. We are a people who wish not to be conquered but rather to live freely, as we have lived since the time of our prophet."

Peucestas repeats her father's sentiments.

Craterus clears his throat. He leans in towards her people. "You have fine horses, Oxyartes."

This man is more real than the others. His speech deeper. His tone less nervous.

Peucestas translates.

"Yes, it is my passion. But you see they reside here with us. They are, if you like, part of the tribe too."

Fahr nods to Shapur, who stokes the brazier with the precision-cut wood that Oxyartes makes them all chop.

"So what can we say to convince you that it is safe for you to come down from this height? That Alexander will treat you well. That you will part of the greatest nation on Earth."

The translator looks at his yellow slippers with the fine gold tips. He fiddles with his sash of bright green. He looks up. He speaks Ptolemy's words.

"There is nothing you can do. We could live up here until we die of natural causes if we choose to do so. We have food, as you can see. We have good beer, much of it; we have enough water always. It is a fine home, this home beneath our God."

Once Peucestas has delivered these words with a finality that suggests the meeting has come to an end, Ptolemy stands. He's angry. She can see that. She looks about his person for any sign that would signal an attack.

Hephaestion states that this is a waste of time. The translator does not translate.

Oxyartes asks his men to stand. Still no words from the Greek translator that dresses as a Persian.

And then her father speaks as the men prepare to walk out of this cave of light and refreshment. "Peucestas—General Peucestas—tell the King of the Macedons that if he wants to take us then he will have to learn how to fly."

She sees the men of her tribe gather to escort the strangers down to the one narrow pathway that will lead them down to their camp below. She sits still, afraid to leave her post, and as she inhales the scent of the oranges she hears the dark general, General Hephaestion, chuckle.

She moves out from her behind the basket when there are no further sounds of footsteps or Greek words. She stretches, and places her arms over her head. The bag of gifts sits there, unopened. She regards it, wondering what it holds.

She does not have to wait too long. Shapur comes to her side and starts to pry open the strings that hold the sides of the bag together. She places an arm on his shoulder and shakes her head from side to side. "No, Shapur. That is for our father to open."

They are about to leave when Bah, her father and Fahr walk in.

Her father sits and places his old head in his hands. "They will move on. The cold is killing them down there."

Her father sends boys in black, faces coloured with kohl, scarves wrapped around their heads to observes the camp below.

"Their supplies?"

Oxyartes scoffs. "Oh, they hunt. They kill our game. Yes, yes, they do that. While we snare little birds to boil in our pots, they roast their kill over roaring fires and the fat and blood drips onto their flames, sending evil smoke into the air above. But these meats, these meals are few and far between sometimes. King Alexander eats, his men eat but others starve. There is no grain. They have wine, but it is kept only for the men of the military.

"Soon there will be sickness for their waters run foul. Their earth is not combed and their waste sits in holes that not even the hungry fly eat."

Fahr sits closer to Roxane. And then her father asks her about the words of the translator. About his friend, Peucestas, as he calls him.

"Father, there was only one part where the words were not a proper translation."

"Go on."

"Well, subterfuge, surprise attacks, and we know you are expert horsemen and hunters." She repeats the words of the nervous Ptolemy.

"And so?" Oxyartes says.

She stutters as she replies. His eyes bore into her. "Father, the words that the translator spoke back to you after Ptolemy spoke were a much kinder version. They were complimentary."

—

"The General Ptolemy was impatient?"

Fahr nods. Bah laughs. Shapur looks towards the bag of gifts.

"Yes, his words were short, curt and with a tone that implied some kind of authority over you."

"I see."

"Let's open that bag," Shapur says.

"Oh, I had entirely forgotten their offerings. Go on, Shapur, see what they bring to us."

It takes no time for Shapur to prize the strings apart, and he takes out the gifts from the Greeks.

On the carpet in front of them he lines up six skulls, all polished, with silver melted into the holes where the eyes and mouths should be.

"They are barbarians, brutal, crude and ..." Oxyartes doesn't finish his sentence.

"Shapur, take these now and put them on the ledge above the forecourt. Leave them there in the hope that Mother Moon might restore some light to these departed souls."

Roxane feels weak. She shakes. She has not eaten. She is thirsty. She stands.

"I will escort you to your cave," Fahr says.

He holds her around the waist as they walk back together. The night is upon them. She stops and holds his hands.

"Bones are the markers of those flown high to the heavens. They are print of a life lived upon the sacred earth. What happened to those people who once wore those skulls, Fahr?"

"He is known for slaughtering. He is known to be inconsistent. He is known to be volatile one time, then calm and kind the next. If someone enrages him, he takes offence and often kills without mercy."

She feels the fear. He holds her head into his shoulder. "But he cannot get us, Roxane. We are safe here. My father and your father have thought of every eventuality. We can survive a very long siege."

He kisses her cheek. And she walks down the remaining steps hewn into this mountainside, to the cave that is calm. Where the pale blue water flows clear. Where the candles give off soft golden light and to where there is a bowl of hazelnuts waiting.

The Military Camp 327 BC

Oh the irony and how it taunts me; bundles of fine silk wrapped and hidden from any kind of ruin. Yet we are near dead.

The tide of a kinder wind is coming. I see my father in this grim half-light. Less gruff. The pull of his hands and around this fire, alone, with all of my tools and wits about me it seems I start to play. For it seems my wits have come to me at last and something else, an energy that burns like my fire and boils like my forge.

I cannot stop my fingers even though they ache. I cannot stop my arms as they hammer smooth the small objects. One foot taps up and down. The dawn comes and goes. The night descends like a shroud around my shoulders.

When I stop, seven silver knives line up like brothers. I polish them and sharpen their blades several times over. I am ready.

You are ready.

My knives are wrapped in a piece of purple silk that I set free from its leather fort. My feet take me to the military camp. It's sheltered in a forest that lies south of the sharp plain on which we camp.

"What's with you lad?" A burly guard draws me to him, pulling at the tattered blanket I wear as a cloak.

"I have some things for the King."

"Let's have a look then." The guard rolls his eyes and turns towards his fellow man who takes the package I offer. The assistant unwraps it with his meaty fingers and

lays the silver implements out on the firelit ground before
him.

They both kneel to take a closer look. The burly
guard places the silver knife shaped like Aphrodite's
body on his hairy forearm and shaves away. His cut hair
falls like dead flies to the ground.

"Oh aye," he says. "For the King."

They wave me through.

Another sentry point, another two guards stand at the
opening of the main tent. It is situated in the middle of the
encampment. We did laundry for these folks, so I have
become familiar with Alexander pitching his tent in the
middle of concentric circles. Most important in the
middle, those of lesser rank on the outside.

This time I wonder if my luck is done. If good
fortune will leave my weary hands.

No ... it won't. It's your time.

It's a voice I do not want to acknowledge,
knowing full well that my head is full of lightness, my
body of little substance, and do not those of a more
sceptical nature say that such a condition renders itself in
delusions? But the voice is instantly recognisable to me.
It's him, my father, the man who gave me life.

So I am waved through once more without even a
second glance. I am in the throngs of the elite. The nobles
and all those who at the end of a day take much wine and
take meat and sing and dance.

I see the courtesan Thais who sits on the lap of
General Ptolemy. They say, or Leo says, that she has
placed a rumour in the minds of those she serves, that
Ptolemy is indeed the late King Phillip's first-born son.
His mother married the noble Lagus, but her nights were
often spent by Phillip's side.

It is hot, too hot. The smells are so strong—oils and fragrance. Sweat, indulgence.

It is General Craterus who sees me first. "Come," he says. "It's quieter out here." He leads me to a little side room where platters of meat sit on a candlelit table. He pours wine and suggests I take some refreshment.

I cannot eat at this time, even though my stomach whines like some kind of stray cat. I drink the wine though. It is not good wine, but it is wine. I know the supply routes have been hard here in the north. Of course they have. We are starving.

"Might I ask who you are?"

"Yes, I am Andronicus, son of Nicodemus, small arms maker to the late Phillip."

"And you bring some arms for us?" says the tall, lean general with shoulder-length fair hair and tanned skin as he regards the purple package I clutch to my side. "The guards suggested that I take a look at them."

"Yes, I do, in fact they are more than small arms, they are …" I try to describe them but am unable, for they are to me a new kind of thing altogether. A new creation born of a dark night beside a roaring fire. From the unknown, patterns that just arrived in my head.

"May I?" Craterus places the silk on the table and unwraps my silver knives.

He takes a long while to respond. I feel suddenly very ill, as though I will vomit up the wine.

Craterus takes each one: the blade that Aphrodite straddles, whose hair is etched in waves down the spine of the knife. A handle of polished wood. She is all but an index finger long and she comes with a scabbard of silver. Then there is the one I have shaped into a slim fish with an eye of jade. Then the one with the little compartment I have made inside the handle. The compartment might take the black gum of the poppy or something secret.

Craterus is placing the blades on his fingertip, seeing how sharp each one is. He is looking closely at them.

The next one he takes is the round one. How odd to have made this. What was I thinking? I feel embarrassed now, as Craterus brings it up close to his face. I have polished it so cleanly that his face will appear on its surface. Its perimeter is very sharp. I made a padded pouch for its head to sit in. The moon, perhaps; maybe I made this one in the image of the moon.

The next one is like a crescent moon. Craterus cleans his fingernails with it. Little debris comes from his nails.

Craterus holds up the serpent. He smiles. The snake-like knife is perhaps my favourite. The whole knife fits into a silver skin. It took the longest to make.

Last is the long poke, for this is what I named it. A slim pick. That is all. A slim pick and nothing else but a handle made of bone. Good for garrotting, good for poking out an eye.

"Andronicus, these are remarkable—quite remarkable."

We are in the King's company. The tent is modest and adjacent to the main tent. Hephaestion is slumped in a chair. A faint whistle comes from his nose as he sleeps. Alexander lies naked upon a Persian couch, his manhood covered only by a scant piece of linen.

"I think we have found, by the good fortune of Zeus who does smile upon his son, Alexander, the man of your imaginings," Craterus says.

Alexander rises up off his elbow and dangles his feet over the side of this slim bed. He looks up and yawns. A eunuch who I did not notice rises. He was stationed in the corner on a footstool of tapestried birds. He is dressed in teal and he pours more wine for the King and the General.

Like Craterus, the King places the small knives on the bed, but unlike Craterus he lines the knives up from tallest to shortest, the poke being the longest, the one with the secret compartment the shortest.

"Craterus, yes, what we spoke of today will be possible." Alexander smiles at Andronicus. "He materializes on the same day we drew up our plans. How is that possible? Oh yes, my father is with me, of course he is, this is proof, is it not, that he dwells with us. Always a hand in what we have to do."

Alexander's presence is mesmerising, his face glows, his words trickle out, ebbing from soft to loud. He looks over to Hephaestion.

"Wake up you lazy bastard. Look what has walked through the door—this man has brought us our wings."

"What?" Hephaestion rouses.

"As Hephaestus made the winged helmet and the winged sandals for Hermes, so this fine craftsmen with make the very things needed to scale that rock."

We are sheltered, warm and fed. We drink wine and hum as we make the small, strong implements that will hold people as they climb up the icy face to the top of the great rock. We live and work in a secret location. My Idahlia, attended by the King's doctor, is well and assists us with the curation of good rope. We are in the company of a team of men recruited for their discreetness and industry.

The Golden Kingdom 327 BC

There are no birds on the flat stones outside. Roxane usually feeds them with the few crumbs of whatever is left in the bottom of their food box, but today they are not waiting, ready to receive their breakfast.

Roxane stands at the portal of their comfortable cave. She looks out to the sunrise that pinks the surrounding hills. It is still, beautifully still.

The snow is clean; there are no prints in its white cloak.

She retreats inside and while Muni and Leila are still asleep, rubs oil of peppermint on her feet, pulls on her woollen socks and boots.

She moves to see the new day, the new world where she thinks of each day as a new beginning. This is something Fahr has taught her. That if one breathes in the light given from heaven, one is restored with an energy that gives rise to joy. Each task must be approached with a belief that you will find the good in everything you do, no matter how large or small the task might be. All else that is in the past lies there, gone.

She rounds the first corner, which will take her up to the forecourt. The air is crisp, as if one could almost eat it or drink it. It is turning. The cold is turning to the gentler spring.

But she is not prepared for what she sees. As she ascends, little lights encircle her. Encircle *them*. Everywhere she looks, lights flicker from silver hats; men stand as still as the old wise tree back in their homeland. Their faces hold no expression. They wear light outfits;

ropes are coiled about their waists and they wear a belt of leather in which she can just make out objects of silver.

Oxyartes, Bah and Fahr are already on the forecourt.

The dawn has passed and the day has begun in earnest. They are all there on the forecourt now, and Oxyartes addresses his people. The women and children are tucked in the centre in neat lines while the men surround them.

"We will soon be taken." Oxyartes' face is as pale as the new snow. "We will no doubt be set free from this world. For we did challenge this King and for that I am sorry. But I do not despair because we will soon reach our summit, the great golden kingdom of our Lord, and as faithful children we will be taken to paradise."

Roxane feels the fear. Even Muni looks frightened. Her mother not so much, for she has courted death for a long time, waiting for it to take her and for her to be released from this cold. A baby cries; it is Fahr's new-born and his wife Simca holds her close and soothes her. Roxane watches this woman kiss her baby's cheek, her face, hold her small chubby hands. Five daughters wait beside the lovely Simca.

Roxane feels something then. A kind of wistfulness, a feeling akin to loss. She will not be a mother. She will never hold a baby in her arms. For today this white hill will run pink with their red blood.

Oxyartes has despatched them back to their caves with food and drink. Everyone, he said, must do what they must in these last few moments of life here on Earth. Her mother pulls on her old brown coat. Muni decides to drink the green drink although she has never touched a drop of it before.

The drink is made far away, in the place where the good spirits congregate when they are not trying to rid the world of evil spirits. The drink is made from wormwood and brewed in big urns under the dark forest's intricate leaves. Roxane has listened as the elders drew straws to see who would be next to travel, to trade their honey and fine figs for the special green drink.

Muni rises and dances and spins. She sings and takes her mother's hand.

"I have loved you, Leila, like I have loved our husband. You are to die with me, we will hold hands and I will fly with you to the above."

Leila starts to drink too, but instead of taking Muni's hand to dance she slumps down by the stream and weeps. "It is not me, not you, Muni, but Roxane that I feel for. I should have …" She trails off. She does not offer any more words. Muni comes to her, embraces her, kisses her. They hold each other.

"Shush, shush. We are sisters. We sit in that hut as our red rain flows, we feel the joy of being a woman. Remember how we all sit there on the ground and it is then that we feel the joy of being a woman. A woman can love, more, remember that," Muni says, and she holds the thin, tall, beautiful woman with the deep brown eyes.

Fahr stands in the door.

Leila points to him. "Fahr, take her and escape." She points to Roxane.

"I have come to borrow her, just for a little while."

"Borrow her, take her," Leila says. "She is yours."

Roxane joins Fahr and he lets her walk in front. He places his hand at the small of her back. "We are going to the cave that we used when the delegation came," he says.

When she enters, Bah and her father are there. They whisper, even though there are no eyes upon them,

---

nor any ears that might hear them. Her father takes her hands. A drop of mucous is about to fall from his nose.

"You, my dear –" He turns away to cough, "are to go to the horses' cave. At the rear of the cave is a slit. Yes, a slit. It is a narrow passage through this opening. But Bah and I have managed it and we are bigger than you my love."

He takes a breath, closes his eyes. "Inside this passage of stone is a way out to the northern side." He pauses again and his hands begin to shake.

"Roxane." It is Bah's voice. Her uncle places an arm around her ageing father. He strokes her father's back. She is frozen to the spot, unable to talk, to speak, to think. It is Fahr who speaks next.

"Roxane, you must walk through this tunnel. It is full of turns and twists and at times you will have to climb up and down. You will have to clamber over rocks and at two points you will need to get down and crawl on your stomach."

He touches her arm. "But do not despair, it is well sourced. Nuts and dried fruits have been placed at good intervals. You will lick the water that runs off the rocks. There are furs to rest upon. Take your time."

Roxane cannot see. She has become blind and deaf. She does not hear the next words.

"Shapur will join you in the stables; this is the first part of this escape."

"What?" she says. She is shivering. "What, no?"

"Yes, you will wait for him to join you before you both disappear."

It seems that she has left her earthly body already. The rock is spinning around her. She begins to fall.

"Give her some of the green drink now," Bah says to his son. He unseals a flask and makes her drink. Her stomach grows warm, as if on fire, and her mind clears, she feels a certain kind of joy. He holds her hand while she recovers.

"Why don't we all go?"

"Because we are known to the men of the Greeks and we are not cowards like King Darius, we will not run."

"Then I will not run."

"But then who will carry on the teachings of our prophet? Roxane, you can already pass as a Greek if you wish. You will be safe and with Shapur, your betrothed, you will have children, many children that will carry on our line," Bah says.

"But they know Shapur."

"We have kept him hidden this morning. He was not at the assembly. Did you notice that?" Fahr says.

She hadn't.

"That was deliberate, and Oxyartes will simply tell Alexander and his men that his son, Shapur, died of a fever."

"But that is a lie. We do not lie."

Oxyartes sighs. "The Good Lord will forgive a lie told to advance his cause, to protect a good life. Now you must go. It is good you are clothed well already. That is all you need. Take nothing else, wait for Shapur in the stables."

"Can I say goodbye to my mother, to Leila?"

"No. No one must know of this plan." Her father turns from her.

"We will all dance in paradise tonight, rest assured," Bah says.

Roxane pleads some more. Fahr takes her hands, leads her out into the sunlight.

"Go," he says.

"But you?"

"Oxyartes should have wed me to you. I have only been allowed one wife. I suspect that is because if Shapur dies then I would be saved for you."

"You have beautiful daughters; they should not die. You should take my place, you and Simca and your seven girls."

Fahr tightens his grip on her. "I have seven daughters; they are not heirs. Now go, Roxane, before the Greeks come and take over this place."

Roxane finds the narrow opening and locates the passage behind. She casts her eye around the cave where the horses live.

She begins to think, to make good on all her thoughts and not to let the reality of what is now, what has happened, swallow her. But it is an impossible task. Her mind keeps going back to those men she saw this morning. A host of fallen stars. She thinks of the man of the west who will soon take their lives. She hopes her father has told him that he must leave their bodies where they fall on the soft snow blanket. That they must go so that the black winged birds can escort them all to the narrow silver bridge. The bridge of judgment. She knows Oxyartes will speak for them all for they have lived a life according to the prophet. That they have kept their word and cared for the place in which they lived.

She feels a deep rush of panic, as if the stone walls are closing in on her, and she makes for the opening. She feels stuck. She feels the fear of being caught between two slabs of stone, the air rushing from her, the feeling of death on her. But what if this is what she is meant to feel? What if, all along, she was to be spared the knife or the rope, or the torture, in order to die in rock. To be pressed together by their home and made one with the rock. Her bones left as reminders that she once lived. That her little birds that she fed each day might find her and lift her soul up to the white clouds and the light beyond.

She manages to calm herself, to breathe deep and free herself. The horses look on. Her favourite animals look on. While waiting here she may as well serve. She will do the job of Fahr and his boys, so at least they and the stable will look well.

She wipes them all down. She combs out the sweat and mud and cleans their eyes of mucous. She places her finger up their noses and wipes away the dust and snot that has collected there. She brings them all warm snow water from the brazier. She rolls up fresh hay and honey and feeds each and every one of them.

She walks to the edge of the cave, pokes her head out. She listens but hears nothing. No screams, no skirmish, no fighting, no cries. From here she cannot see the guard of the men who surrounded them overnight. She can only see below, where once her people thrived. *Strong bones and strong blood make a good people.*

Unbearable waiting. She sweeps out the stable using an old broom she used as a girl. A mix of chaff and wood crumbs, a few dry leaves, precious used and messed hay. She collects it all and places it an alcove used to store the muck. Muck that will be used later, on crops or to nourish a hungry field.

She spreads out fresh matting. The smell of the wood dust is nice. The smell of the new hay is nice. The crunch of old dry leaves is too much, for it makes her deaf to what might be going on above her. She stops and treads softly, pacing back and forth, kissing each horse on its nose.

On a normal day, what would they do next?

They would walk the horses, as much as it is possible on this rock. But no, she can't do that today. So

79

she begins to stroke Minoo, her horse, who she speaks odd nothings to.

There is noise. Loud noise. Slapping noise. Leather on stone. Beating. A beating of her people. But then it grows louder until it is nearly with her.

She grabs Minoo and pulls her out from her tether. She leaps behind her and pulls Minoo towards her. She hides like she hid once before, with her spine pressed hard into the rock. She drops her head low, stills her beating heart and listens some more.

But then the noise abates. She is in agony.

She comes from behind Minoo's rump and sits on the new bed of hay and leaves and chips. She puts her hands in front of her eyes. She finds her mouth moves, as Phaidros' mouth once moved when he taught them the poem *Hymn to Aphrodite* by the great poet Sappho. She finds peace here. She finds herself pretending to be her old Greek tutor. The way his body moved in a kind of sway as he recited verse, or a story that he had learnt off by heart. Off by heart, such a curious expression. She would have been inclined to say set in her mind, so one would not forget.

She finishes the last line. *Come to me once more, and abate my torment; take the bitter care from my mind and give me all I long for; lady, in all my battles fight as my comrade.*

She waits again, urging her brother to hurry up. *Hurry up.* Those familiar words that she spoke to him all the time when he walked slow, when he rode slow, when he spoke slow.

There is a cloud outside; this happens sometimes when it is still, the mist lowers like a veil. A wet mist that makes it seem as if you are walking through smoke.

Slap, slap, voices, the steps outside, reverberating with thumps, and men's voices.

She does not have time to walk to the crevasse in the rock. She tries to run but the sound is upon her.

She ducks behind Minoo again and pulls her horse friend close to her, shuffling her so that her rump covers all her body and the stone is sharp behind.

"Your horses, Oxyartes, some say are the finest anyone has ever seen."

She hears the echo of the translator, Peucestas. Then she hears her father. His voice is so much stronger than it was this morning.

"We breed good horses. They are of good speed, good health, good blood, good bone and good temperament."

The gathering of men whisper and chat in Greek. She can't see the faces, nor the bodies, but she can see their feet.

A pair of toes stops beneath her. Open-toed sandals in this very cold climate. Yet the feet are not blue, nor wizened. The nails are not damaged or black.

"Well, Oxyartes," the voice says, "you have really excelled here."

She sees her father's soft black boots appear beside the very good toes.

"Oh, Minoo, yes, she is a very good example of our finest. The product of a beautiful Arabian stallion and a very charming and sweet steppe pony."

"And she has six legs."

Over Minoo's rump a soft pair of blue eyes appear. Roxane lifts her head to meet them and then something in this room of grey rock seems to pause, as if time has slowed, slowed like a river turning to ice.

A hand reaches for her, and she is pulled from behind the horse to the centre of the cave room.

"Well, Oxyartes, I would have hidden her too, if she were mine."

"Roxane, my daughter, she loves horses you know. So that is where she went. To the stable, and it seems she has cleaned it already—fed them too."

"Would someone please fetch her a cape or a cloak, or even a blanket—she is shivering," the man who must be Alexander says.

So they are not dead, they have not been slaughtered, or captured, tied up, or pushed off the rock to their death. Her father seems to be in good spirits. Bah at the back smiles at her.

The man she knows as the General Craterus walks forward and takes off his cloak. He places it around her shoulders. "Alexander," he says, "I believe this maiden here does speak our tongue."

"Really?"

"Yes. I heard it from her mother, the beautiful Leila born of the roses."

"Well, I command that you speak to us in the tongue of our forebears, who gave us speech and reason."

Roxane feels all the eyes upon her. She remembers Phaidros' face. She conjures it up and places it before her. She pretends he is just there, right in front of her. Roxane begins.

"He takes a spear and pierces the ground, slicing the salty soil with the tip of gold. And as he cried his clear tears, his mother did come to him. Thetis rose right before him from the deep blue sea. Achilles rests his head on her shoulders; she wears the flowers of the sea upon herself. She smells both of forest and sea. *He should not have gone against the Gods*, Achilles whispers into his mother's soft ear. *He took my armour. He took it and was killed by Hector. Hector mistook him for me*. Achilles sobs. *Now I must avenge his death*. Thetis weeps. She wishes she could wrap her son's head in the plants of the sea to cool it. She releases her grip on him. All but his heel is covered in her immortal gift. She pleads with her

son, *Oh but wait one more day*. For to act in anger, means
judgment is impaired. To rush in causes even the wisest
to fault. Thetis thinks of Zeus who in anger cast out
Hephaestus. It is she that now cares for Hephaestus,
soothes all his aches and pains. She does this in the
hollow of a cave in which a stream runs through. She
watches over the great smith of the Gods."

Alexander claps.

Then there is more clapping.

Muni says no one ever leaves the Baron's lands. "Never."
She sits by the stream, her eyes red. Roxane cannot bear
to look at her puffy face, caused by the tears she shed
overnight.

Leila is holding up her silk dresses, swishing them
this way and that. Roxane has no interest in trying any of
them on.

Instead she sits by the brazier and gazes into the
flame as if the fire will provide the answers.

"He cannot take you; you are promised already,"
Muni says.

"None of that matters now, Muni," Leila says.
"He is our new leader and she is to be his wife."

"He has no other wife, no children. A man of that
stature should have taken his own breed to be his. No not
our one."

"But she is of royal blood. Oxyartes said that
himself at the meeting with Alexander. You were there,
Muni, you heard it. Roxane's bloodlines were revealed to
Alexander when he called for a meeting with Oxyartes
and his close circle to ask for her hand in marriage. Cyrus
the Great's line extends to Rohan her grandfather, and so
it passes through her too. The greatest King of all, that
was how Alexander described Cyrus."

"But she is promised. No one breaks a promise made to God."

"On this occasion, Muni, it ensures we survive."

"Oh, you should know how cruel it is to be traded."

"Shush." Roxane stands. "As my mother says, Muni, I am sad, I am fearful, I am …" No more words will come. She waits till she catches her breath. "I am strong."

"Strong enough to give birth to heirs for Oxyartes. That is what is needed, not for you to be traipsed around the world in the name of bloodshed and greed," Muni says.

"Were you not traded too, Muni? Come on, tell us all. From the impoverished nothingness of the northern steppes. Ponies and a wife," Leila says.

"No, I was glad to come, to be allowed to leave, and I bore Oxyartes a son."

"We are all only wombs and Roxane is just another womb to another man wanting an heir. But I am happy with that, for she will leave the cold and the confines of this place and she will experience what neither of us will ever experience," Leila says.

"And what might that be?"

"To be held by a handsome man, to be cherished, to be adored because she is the most beautiful woman that he has ever seen. He called her the Helen of the North."

"Stop it, both of you!" Roxane shouts. She pours her mother a measure of the green drink and then places her arm around Muni. "It would seem our one true God has spoken. And in order for you all to thrive beyond what you know now, I go willingly."

She bites on the word *willingly*, for at the moment it is a lie. But soon, with her thoughts and her might, she will turn that into the truth. She is working on it, moment by moment, as she sits in front of that fire.

It is late in the day when Fahr appears at the door to the cave. The spring is creeping back to winter, the sleet and the rain pushes down on them. Their only sanctuary is the cave.

Behind Fahr is a small man, a eunuch. He wears a peacock-coloured ensemble and the feathers in his turban are soggy; his silk teal breeches and jacket are soaked. Muni drags him towards the fire, mothering him as if he were a young puppy.

The eunuch examines the silk dresses that Muni places before him on the clean stone floor. "They are a little moth eaten," he says, "but what does it matter? By the time she reaches the altar and the Magi, the men will have had their fill of wine and beer and will be blind to it."

He picks the green one. "Matches her eyes."

Muni hangs up the chosen dress. "The tent is being erected, even in this most devilish of weather. And it will have a floor, so that she can dance without having stone underfoot. A magi has been sent for and the ceremony will happen tomorrow night."

"In the dark," Muni says

"Yes, night-time." The eunuch fusses over the rest of the details with the two mothers. Roxane is content to look on; she places her hand discreetly into Fahr's warm one.

"What if I don't want to live royally? What if I want to live here?"

"And marry Shapur?"

Roxane holds her tongue. She sighs.

"You were born royal, Roxane," he says.

Soon enough Muni is lining stones up on the ground—stones that will remind her of what she must do tomorrow to prepare her bride. The eunuch has enchanted her, and even in his abrupt and rude way she has found some humour in it. They exchange kisses on both cheeks

———

and Fahr collects the little man and they turn into the cold again.

Roxane does not sleep. She thinks, and the thinking will not stop. She chastises herself. How can she imagine when she knows nothing outside the land of Oxyartes. Scenes flash in and out of her mind: rivers, the sea, shells, forests, monsters; mostly born from the mouth of Phaidros. Imaginings of what she might experience. But it is fruitless and beguiling to do this. She sits up and rubs her eyes, and pleads with her one true God to take these notions away from her. She must instead think only on her composure. On choosing the right words, the right thoughts. The thoughts that will arm her in this new life.

She rakes her mind to think what these might be. She imagines waking at the start of a day. She will be silent, listen, observe. She will only speak if she has something worthy to say. She must eat well in order to be strong. She must not drink spoiled water; she must treat everyone as though they mean something to her. For even if at first this is a lie, it will eventually become true for she will make friends, allies.

She will ask if she may hunt. She will do as her husband bids, for even though she had only a few sessions in the hut of red rains back down in their fields, she did learn the way of touch. How to run a hand over the body of your loved one. How to give pleasure and how to receive pleasure.

The day is long. Too long. Roxane walks out to seek some relief, but Muni says that a bride must remain hidden until she is called for. To see one's bride on the so-called marriage day would bring bad luck. Despite the

teachings of their prophet on omens and fortune-telling
and superstition, Muni still holds firm to her ways. She
cannot help herself. And in the realm of the dusty days
and cold nights, it was always Roxane that reminded her
of the evil spirits and the good spirits. "Draw the good
spirits close, Muni, and they will protect you from
anything evil."

Her mother suffers the usual headache. Roxane
makes her drink copious amounts of the water, cooled
and flavoured with mint.

"I am feeling better now. Just the shock of you
going. But I know this is better for you, my Roxane. This
is how you … we should –" But she pauses on the word
should, looks up at her daughter, brushes her cheek with
her cold hand. "Yes, you will return to what is ours."

Muni sleeps in the afternoon. Her snores echo in
the chambers of their cave. Leila takes Roxane's hand
and walks to the front of the cave where the little birds
hover. Roxane has no crumbs for them, instead she lets
them nibble on her forefinger.

"Roxane, of Rohan, of Cyrus, of my mother who
was born noble and came from the house of Artaxerxes."
She coughs into a linen. "You see, I was the youngest of
all my sisters. I watched them as suitors came to our court
and I watched as my father chose husbands for them. One
by one they left our court, and returned with their young
children."

Roxane takes her mother's hand.

"Well, you see, my father liked fine things. Roses,
of course. We made oils from those roses; we dried the
petals for bowls that would grace royal and noble houses.
We picked them fresh, and traders would come and take
them in their barrows to sell at markets. My father also
liked the best incense. Not just the sandalwood that
Oxyartes uses to purify our souls, but also that of amber,
patchouli, frankincense, jasmine. Oh Roxane, our house

—

smelt beautiful, all the time. He liked fine drink. No beer, none of the green drink of the fairy women; no—he would take the lions' milk brewed by the nomads that often came to take shelter around our great buildings. He liked dates, he liked figs and pomegranates, all of which these friendly transient people would trade for some of his precious oil. And he liked fabrics, silks, fine linens and the woven carpets."

Leila looks out, the day is clearing. She smiles and points to the parting clouds, the glimpses of light. "It will come good for you tonight, Roxane, God is smiling on you."

There is a pause and then Leila speaks again. "I'm not married yet, not even promised to anyone. I heard my mother say that as the youngest I would be the one to stay. There were no sons, you see, so my father chose the eldest grandson to inherit his place." A tear runs free from her mother's deep brown eyes. "I met this handsome man once, a trader. When you see a handsome man it does turn your heart. He and I took the night together."

"And?"

"Roxane, it was wonderful."

"And the trader?"

"He left before I even woke. I looked for him again but did not ever see him. Not long after that Oxyartes visited my father in search of a stable in which to shelter his new stallion and himself."

A light snow falls. "Little rose petals, see?" Leila says, laughing, collecting some in her hand. She sniffs back more tears. "My father, he had noticed that my stomach had blossomed. To me it seemed only a little raised. It was hardly noticeable, but my father has a nose for these things. He called for me while Oxyartes was with him in his fine salon. I stood before Oxyartes, the Baron of the north."

"Did Oxyartes ask to marry you?"

"No, my father gave me to him in exchange for the fine stallion he had found in the south."

Roxane feels her own tears spilling on that new snow.

"Do not cry, my love." Leila allows some more flakes to settle in her hand. "Little stars. You know that Roxane means Little Star. I called you that."

"What happened to the trader?"

"I don't know, my darling. But I loved him. Even though it was just one night I loved him more than I have loved anyone besides you. But this was my destiny, my path, and I have you. And even though I cry at your departure, I know you return to the place where you are meant to live."

"I was born in Sogdia?"

"Yes. Muni made me my brown coat so it would seal your beginnings inside and give no one cause to … suspect, if you like. It was a difficult birth, and she would allow no one in. She bolted the door while I laboured and she gave you life, as much as I gave you life. And when I held you, and saw the dark hair, the shape of your face, and when later you opened your eyes and they turned green—well, they are his eyes, Roxane."

They walk up to the forecourt, much like they walked up the incline to Roxane's betrothal; Muni in front, Roxane behind, and Leila further back. The snow is gentle and with the big flares that the Greeks have set all around the rock it makes the snow look like a sunrise.

Leila stops, falls on her knees. Roxane and Muni look back. "Oh stop your sobbing girl, we have finished our grieving, now it's time to wish joy." Muni says, hurrying back to her friend.

But Leila is not crying, she has vomited. A pool of green lies in the snow. A lake of green.

Roxane cleans her mother's mouth and they continue.

The tent is gigantic. It looms and rises over their meeting place. Roxane must make her entry alone, for this was the eunuch's instructions. Guards stand either side of her as she is let into the great pavilion. She sees the aisle she must walk down, and decides not to look either side of her; instead she will walk towards the waiting Magi.

The service runs before her, she hears no words, she only feels Alexander's hands in hers. He has warm hands. The sea of people, the river of life, it is rushing and deafening and her legs shake.

Alexander leads her down the aisle to a side tent. It is well-made, lined with furs and on the raised floor are many cushions; a vessel holds a blood-red liquid.

There is no blanket held by four elders, as there would be if these were her own people. A blanket that the bride would crouch down and follow her new husband under, before consummating their marriage for all to hear.

Instead, she finds herself sitting on a plump red cushion in the shielded tent where she believes no one can see her or her husband. Where their voices if low will go unheard. Alexander stares into her eyes and declares her the most beautiful woman he has ever seen. He kisses the top of her head and offers her wine.

"Drink; it will help," he says.

So she does. The liquid is smooth and sweet.

"I had my cup bearer mix up a special batch just for you. Do you like it?"

The drink has warmed her insides, and she feels some of the terror leave her. Alexander waits till her cup is empty. He pours himself another; she declines a second cup.

She waits for the inevitable. It is just the two of them and she is grateful that no witness is present to watch the fusing of their flesh, for she has heard many a times how the act is not pleasant the first time and how the women of her tribe found that the wedding night was not intimate at all.

Alexander asks that she is patient, that she steadies him when he gets overexcited. "You see, I am hasty, it's my worst fault."

She smiles. "Do you like the works of Sappho?"

He lifts an eyebrow. "Why yes, I do."

"When I am in doubt, I reach for her words; my tutor taught me her verse."

"Say it to me, speak some words from the poet herself."

"*There is no place for grief in a house which serves the Muse. What is beautiful is good, and who is good will soon be beautiful. Someone, I tell you, in another time will remember us. You came and I was longing for you.*" Roxane whispers, her eyes looking down towards her toes. Alexander lifts up her chin.

"From the poem 'If Not Winter'. Truly sublime," Alexander says.

Alexander pauses a minute and then places a finger in the dimple on his chin; a little cup in his chin.

She notices this; she notices how blue his eyes are. She smells his hair, fresh from washing.

"So I'm going to do this. It will be our secret. For no one but us to know."

He takes a small silver object out of a pocket within his cloak. She sees a woman's body wrapped around the stem of the handle. He removes the blade from its scabbard. Then he draws up the pleats of his leather skirt and slices his thigh. His fingers squeeze the wound so that droplets of blood form. He nods to her.

She withdraws the stained cloth from her breastbone and he collects the blood. Then he cuts the laces of that tent with the same tiny knife and tosses the cloth outside.

They hear a cheer, a thumping of feet upon a wooden floor. They see the Magi take the cloth and close his eyes in prayer.

Bactria 327 BC

 On this most pleasant and sunny day I notice a stranger
across the way from us. She holds a willow basket. Out of
the corner of my eye I continue to watch her while
polishing a silver rabbit, a trinket that I have made.

She ventures towards me, this woman, who looks
neither Persian nor Greek.

"Are you Andronicus?"

"Yes."

"General Craterus told me to find you, for he says
that you and your wife might be able to help us."

"Idahlia, we have a visitor," I call out to my
beloved, who at this time of day likes to rest.

I take our guest inside, for it is shady and cool
there and Idahlia has set up our tent nicely. I have
pretended not to notice the coin that Idahlia has spent on
lavish furnishings and fittings.

"I'm Sarah, handmaiden to the new Queen."

"Many do not view her as the Queen," Idahlia
says. "And if it is laundering you are after, we don't do
that anymore."

"No, it is not laundering—no, no, it is dressing."

Idahlia stills. She holds her tummy. "Then you
have come to the right place."

"We do have some good-quality silk," I say.

"The General did mention this, and he said that
you –" she turns towards my wife, "– Idahlia, isn't it?
That you once dressed Roxane's mother-in-law. That
your stitch is fine and worthy of this travelling court."

"We will need her measurements," Idahlia says.

"I took the liberty of bringing you these." Sarah lifts the lid on her basket and puts a pile of different-coloured ribbons, all folded up, in front of us. Then she takes a sheet of folded parchment. She places this on our small table and unfolds it to reveal a drawing of a woman. A tiny piece of each ribbon is pinned to a body part.

Idahlia screws up her face.

I unfurl the ribbons and imagine this shape. "It's fine, Idahlia, it's fine, we can make the garments up to fit."

"I am not convinced," Idahlia says. "It would be better to measure her in person. To gauge all her faults that need hiding."

"I just need you to tell me three more things," I say.

"Yes, please, Andronicus. I will answer if I can."

"Tell me the colour of her eyes, the colour of her hair, and the colour of her skin."

A full moon cycle has come and gone and I have yet to package up the garments. We have worked day and night to make these clothes. And it seems as if the handmaiden Sarah was happy for us to design what we liked.

I decided to augment the garments with gemstones purchased at the local market, with the silver and gold that fills our chest once again. Alexander has paid us well for our efforts under the Sogdian Rock.

Idahlia is moody. Resistant. I excuse this behaviour because she is growing our child. I believe this is the prerogative of expectant mothers. She craves nuts, of all things, and I am forever marching up and down to the vendors along the alleyway from our tent to purchase yet another round of fine almonds, or walnuts. And on this diet of nuts and much fatty meat my wife has grown quite large. I say nothing, for it is better to have a bit of meat on the bones; I imagine this is particularly good when there is a baby on the way.

Idahlia has no energy to help me package up the clothes, so I take each garment and hold it up one last time; the dark green silk is a long flowing Grecian gown, caught under the bust in a thin sash of the same green. I have chosen pearls to go with this outfit, and I have made earrings of a single pearl drop, and a string of pearls for her neckline.

The dark blue silk was most suited, I thought, to a long cloak. I lined it with pink silk. I placed small pockets into its seams, and placed a comb that could pin up her hair into one of the pockets. I chose silver, with cut slivers of polished glass.

The only chiton we made was of the orange silk, a plain tunic with a belt of black leather. I fashioned a scarf for her out of white wool, and bought large bangles carved out of bone from a local jeweller.

The white silk we made into a long gown with an overlaid coat. Idahlia, with her fine stitching, made a top stitch over the stitch underneath. She pulled some of the wider fabric together so it formed a narrow ribbing, and sewed a light green ribbon over the breast. I watched my wife as she caught the hem up so that the gown had many layers.

And so I fold, admiring my wife's fine work and quietly complimenting myself on how the designs have taken shape. Idahlia did manage to find a woman in our civilian encampment who was similar in size to the measured-out ribbons.

We receive no comments from the citadel after the clothes are delivered. We receive a bag of gold delivered by one of the pages. My wife becomes dejected. She would like to at least set eyes on this girl. Does she even exist? There is much speculation in the camp.

"A barbarian, ugly, bear-like."

"She is cursed."

"Why didn't he marry a Greek princess?"

"She is vulgar and unsuitable."

We carry on in Bactria. It is not an unpleasant place, and the talk flies in our baggagers' camp, for we have heard that Alexander plans to continue his crusade and take us to India. He will convert that place, that magical place, as he calls it, to the ways of the Greeks. Paradise lies beyond the four rivers of that land and once there we will then take the trade routes off those filthy Arabians who tell such tall tales in order to put off others who might covet those waters. Islands of fire that spit and burn a face. Birds whose beaks are so large they can swallow a man whole. Currents that rise up like the great mountains that lie to the very north, the sea wide and wild, swallowing everything in its path.

It is this talk that feeds us. We wait, expectantly. Idahlia is not opposed to going further; she says she wants our child to be raised in a free world, not subjected to servitude. We suit this world, she tells me.

"Andronicus, Idahlia." It is a welcome voice; it is that of the handmaiden. She stands outside our tent in the late sun, holding the same basket. "Can I trouble you? I have brought some things for you."

Idahlia stands aside so she can pass into our over-furnished tent. I have no idea how we will get these things into our carts. It riles me. I am not a man of fuss. I prefer to keep things simple.

"Would you like some wine?" I say.

"Yes, just a little." Sarah notices in one corner the small garments that Idahlia has made. Idahlia follows her eyes. "Did you make these for the court? I can see that you have used the remnants of the cloth you so carefully and beautifully used on my mistress."

"They are not for her or you." Idahlia says. She strides to the pile of baby clothes and moves them in one sweep to the rear of our tent.

"I'm so sorry." Sarah puts a hand to her mouth. "Sometimes I say things without thinking. I am so sorry Andronicus."

I raise my hand to placate her. "It's just … my wife is pregnant. But you cannot really tell, for she has gained… you know."

"Oh I am so happy for you both! I am a midwife, like my mother before me. That is partly why I am assigned to Roxane, the Queen. So if you need any assistance at the birth, please call on me. Or before, if you are worried about any little thing."

"We won't need your help," Idahlia shouts from the back. "If you could leave whatever is in the basket and return to your high house, that would be preferable."

Sarah's eyes well up. "Look, it is just a few nicknacks that I brought with me from the court of Artabazus. For that is where I live most of the time." She extracts a box made of ebony inlaid with ivory in which is stored some incense. She places some precious nutmegs on the table. "So good with a little butter, grate a little into soft butter and place on chicken. I would say fish too, but we are far from the sea."

She stands to leave.

I mouth a thank you to her."How is the Queen?" I ask, trying to stop her from leaving, for she might know more about what is happening inside the military camp. Just yesterday we heard of a revolt, of the pages, stopped only by Fida, the Syrian Seer, who warned Alexander. Many pages were hanged after this.

"Oh, she is homesick. She is missing riding and hunting. And she is not unfortunately carrying a child. I would have maybe expected this to have happened, but of course how can it happen when …" she trails off. "The wine, it has carried off my tongue again. If anything, I must be discreet and now I have …"

"Your words are safe with me. We have no need to speak of this."

"So he does not fuck her? Is that what you are saying? For it is well known that he finds women repulsive," Idahlia says, coming out of the recess beyond.

She picks up the few items Sarah has placed on our table, her face twisted. "We laboured hard for that barbarian girl, and for what?"

"She looks beautiful—even more beautiful in the garments you made for her, Idahlia. You are fine craftsmen and women."

"*Seamstress*. Well at least the courtesans appreciate our work."

I am taken aback, for we do not do any work for the courtesans, apart from the laundering we once did for them. And of course they paid us nothing for that service. Thais, the head courtesan, did ask if we could fashion her some jewellery like that we sent up the hill to Roxane. And make her some silk gowns with the few bolts we had left. But I said to Idahlia, who was all set to do it, that we must see payment first.

Sarah picks up her empty basket and walks out the fold of our door. I follow her.

"I am so sorry for Idahlia. But you see the heaviness of the baby, and such. It is taking a toll. And the uncertainty of where we will head next," I whisper.

"I understand better than most. The body does transform quickly, the mind is slow to adapt. We must cater to the mother's needs always."

"You speak good Greek," I say to her as we walk up the alley way.

She smiles back. "The great Artabazus sought exile at the court of Phillip. As my mother was the midwife at the exiled court, I accompanied the family to the city across the sea. We lived at the court. Alexander was never far away. We ate as a family. Phillip was very generous to my master. We learnt Greek, for none of the Greeks could speak our tongue." She laughs, her light olive skin glowing in the sunset. Her eyes are dark, almond shaped. Her hair is curled into a tight knot at the back of her head.

"If I might ask?"

"Yes, of course."

"Do you know for where we are headed? *Really* headed?"

She nods her head. "Yes, we are to split into two groups. One will journey up to the rooftop of the world. North—far north, where the mountains are so high they merge with the clouds and the blue of the paradise. The other will take the lower pass into India." She pauses. "Alexander has only chosen a few men to accompany him in the first group. He believes he will meet his father, Zeus Ammon, there. We are to travel behind General Hephaestion. We will all meet up in a place called Taxila."

Theo's tent is in front of us. The smell of braised meat wafts out. Rosemary and fresh marjoram. Theo beckons us. "Come try, Andronicus, and bring your lady friend. I have a dish for you."

Theo, the cook, and his wife Sybilla pull out chairs for us and we sit at a table away from the rest of the diners. Theo, who I have helped often with the fashioning of fine platters and cups, tells us he is honoured to have us as guests. "I tell you often, Andronicus, come dine with us, but you do not come. But today you come."

We drink their wine. It is not so watery. It is a thicker blend.

"You should get back to Idahlia," Sarah says.

"She needs to rest."

"Can I speak with you boldly?" Sarah asks, placing a linen from her sleeve onto her lap. "I feel I can trust you."

I nod.

"The citadel is not as many imagine, for it crumbles and was full of dust and leaves and goodness knows what when we arrived there. Old and in great disrepair. But I digress. We manage well enough. I have six houseboys to assist me on loan from my master. But, Andronicus, it is very isolating."

The plates of food arrive, steaming, and the aromas make my mouth water. Sarah stares at the food. I wait for her to begin to eat.

"Smells good?" I say.

"Yes; very often I serve. Seldom am I waited on these days."

"Do you not have cooks in the big house?"

"No, just the houseboys whom I teach to become better houseboys. Better men in a world that is changing." She begins to eat. "I am talking too much, but I did mean what I said, can I speak to you frankly?"

I nod. "Go on, yes."

"It seems to me that many view Roxane, the Queen, as someone who is dull in wit, devoid of intelligence, ugly. I can assure you she is anything but."

"She lived on a rock in the wilderness," I reply. "We have not set eyes on her. There is no reason to view her as anything other than a peasant."

Sarah shakes her head. "Andronicus, she is the strangest woman I have ever met but she is no fool."

I eat.

"I tell you now two things; you must promise you will not share this with anyone. Most particularly your wife, although please encourage Idahlia to not think of Roxane as a savage but as a woman worthy of her royal status."

I nod in agreement, enjoying this food. Food without accompanying complaints.

"Number one, and this I find very curious. You see, the King has only visited her the once. In all this time he leaves a fertile young woman of great beauty and mind, alone, in a run-down abandoned fort."

"Well, he has much to plan, to do, if he is to conquer India and beyond."

"Yes, that was the excuse he made when he did visit the once. And it was on this occasion that I came to notice how very different Roxane was."

I push the wine towards her.

"He arrived late, not seen by anyone, not heard by us; he was just there, seated on the outside terrace at the back of the building. I panicked. I had not drawn a bath, nor laid up a marital bed. I had little to serve him in the way of food. But he did not seem to mind about any of that."

I listen, enthralled, honoured even that she should tell me all this.

"He asks that his wife sit with him outside, for the air is warm. So I quickly dress her in the white silk, for it does suit her well and is something that a princess might wear to the bedroom. I accompany her out and take my place inside the small inset where I can be sure to be on hand should they need anything, anything at all.

"I see him pass her something. It sits there on the small table between them. It's a rock, Andronicus, a plain old grey rock about the size of an orange."

I finish eating and push my plate aside. She has only eaten about a quarter of her meal. She also pushes her plate aside. "Then," she says, "he asks her what she makes of it, this rock. She takes it and places it under the lamp. She rolls it around looking at it from all sides. 'There is a small fish in it. And the imprint of perhaps a shell,' she says. He tells her he found the rock on the banks of the River Oxus. He asks her how the fish and the shell-like pattern came to be in the rock. She takes her time, Andronicus, but she replies. 'Rivers, we know something of them. That the mud in them can harden and become rock. We have dropped buckets at times into their shallow purity, careful not to disturb, and hauled out mud that my father instructed boys to make into bricks. So mud hardens.' She stopped there but he told her she must continue with her thoughts. 'So eventually maybe the mud hardens into rock and the fish from the river and the shell from the river got stuck in the mud that eventually turned to stone.' This is how she answered him."

"What happened next? Was he pleased with her answer?"

"I couldn't tell, but he asked her, what if the shell imprint was made by a seashell; what if the fish was not from the river itself but from the sea?"

"And?"

"It took her some moments to answer him, but she did. 'Maybe God was very displeased at one time, and he cried many tears in sadness, so many tears that the basin in which his tears are collected, the sea, overflowed and these tears of sadness had nowhere else to go but up the rivers and the fish and the seashells were carried along in the flood of the rivers"

I sit back, breathe out. "A flood so big—it happens, does it not? We know it, you and I—well I assume you do, when a river bursts its banks due to heavy rain."

Sarah laughs. "Andronicus, I wouldn't have been able to think of this, nor would I have been able to hold my composure. Standing there in that small alcove I was more nervous than she was."

She drops her head, folds up her linen and replaces it in her pocket. I can tell there is something else she wants to say. I don't press her, but I stay in case she wants to add something further.

She takes one last sip of wine; her cup is empty. I offer to walk her back to the citadel for it is getting dark.

"No, Andronicus, do not worry, I know that there are already eyes and ears on me. But thankfully none inside this hospitable tent, for I recognise all of those sent to keep us safe, free from harm. And I made sure I was facing away from them so they could not make out my words." She leans down. "That night after they had discussed the rock, he simply stood up, kissed the top of her head and made his way down the path. Strange, is it not?"

It is some days later that Alexander finally calls an assembly. He stands on a dais with Hephaestion. "We are to follow in the footsteps of the great Heracles. Some of us will walk where he walked, on a mountain, high with the Gods. Some will travel a kinder path. Both journeys will take us to Taxila, where my great friend and ally, the Rajah Abisares, will make us welcome.

"There is only one Rajah in the whole of India that opposes us. It is not the good Rajah Abisares, but the Rajah Poros. And we will overcome him and then we will

——

ford the four rivers of this land and stand on a coastline that will mark the beginning of a new world.

"And I am building a new city to honour this new world. It is being built as we speak. It lies on the rim of the blue sea, and it will be called Alexandria of Egypt.

"We will become a united nation of peoples. And I, like you, will dance with the Gods."

The speech is short and the sun hot. I make my way back to the shade of our tent, to drink cool water and eat some melon. Idahlia is lying on our rug. I see that her body is not just swollen in the belly but in her legs as well. Her face, her upper arms. She breathes with much noise.

I tap her and she startles. "So, what did he say?"

"What was expected, except for one thing. That he is building another Alexandria, this time in Egypt and it will be the centre of his world."

"Well, Egypt is good, Andronicus, we could live there in a grand house. We could have servants and we could raise our children there."

"It is a fine country, my love." The temple in Siwah where Alexander made his pilgrimage is still much spoken about in our circles. We discuss much about his journey there in the alleyways of this camp, in all the other camps we have pitched our tent in. It was the place where his godly origins became known. Where the seer there predicted, less favourably to our King's ears, that he would be the first of three great kings. But she did say that he would change the world for ever. For good or bad? That is what some of us wonder now. For some say he is turning into a tyrant.

But at this moment I am more concerned with my love, whose face is red, whose hair is dry and brittle and whose breath smells hot and odd. I place cool water beside her. She drinks it down and then I cut up melon into small pieces and place them in her mouth.

That night a wind starts up; a rowdy wind that shifts the sides of our tent. I peg them down with more nails, hammering and hammering until the sides do not move from the ground, but still the walls move in and out, creaking with the rage of this tempest. Soon the dust finds ways into our home. Red dust. Gritty dust.

And then Idahlia moans, she retches. She is in pain. I say we must seek help, but she bats me with a hand and tells me that the child will be hers and hers alone. I do not argue with this. Perhaps she has gone back to her own birth, where as a child she was taken from her mother and given to the old washerwoman.

I mop her brow. She says to me it is time, time for the child. She groans with each sharp pain.

Time passes and I cannot leave her to her suffer any longer. I lift her up, heave her into my arm. I hold her while I fumble with the tent's lacings. The wind whips us, the sand scratches. I make her walk out into the alleyway. We seek shelter when we exhaust ourselves, behind anything that is solid and wide. She is getting worse. I place her feet upon my own and walk for two.

Eventually I see the hill on which sits the great fort, the citadel. I stagger up the path. The wind gives us no respite. Our hair, our lips, our mouths are full of dust.

I knock on that door. I knock again, this time using my fists.

The door opens just enough for the person on the other side can see who it might be.

"I'm Andronicus," I puff and wheeze at the face that appears. "We need Sarah's help."

The door opens just enough to let us in.

The candles flickers over the face of a goddess. "Athena, Athena," I say. I am delusional, the herculean effort has made me see double, has made me wistful. I am relieved to be safe inside, safe from the torment of this formidable wind.

"Come," the girl says, and she leads us into a large spacious room. She helps me lower my wife onto a couch. She runs off and returns with Sarah, who is wearing a pink nightgown which she covers up with an old black shawl. Her hair is springy.

Sarah examines my wife, as she groans and flails on the bed. "Hold her still, Roxane, so I can feel her tummy."

I can sense Sarah's anguish, her worry.

"Save her, please. Save her," I plead.

"She is too early, Andronicus. She has a sickness which puts her life at risk. The baby may be dead already, for this disease is deadly. I'm so sorry."

"What can you do?"

Roxane comes to Idahlia; she places her hands on my wife's forehead. "When the ewes were in strife, we helped them with our hands."

Sarah looks over to the calm Roxane. She straightens. "Yes, we must do everything possible. Everything we know must be used."

Roxane begins to light candles, many of them on a large metal frame. She puts wood on the large fireplace. She runs out of the room, calling after her that she will get the black paste, the linens, the towels and Sarah's bag of instruments.

Sarah guides me through the massive wooden doors and down a long passageway. She places me in a room with cushions and view of the dark, windswept night. She claps her hands, and as if by magic several boys come to her side.

"I need to get to work now, Andronicus, the boys will take care of you."

I lie down on the cushions. I do not want to sleep. I need to be awake for Idahlia, for anything she might want of me. But I know that in this moment I am useless. What use is gold, or silk, what use is coins? What use is fire, even?

I wake to the sound of cups on saucers. One of the boys has poured me a mint tea. And as the dawn shatters the horrible night, the boys pray. They sit in a circle, near the large window around a rug of deep. Their winged God watches them from the centre of this red world. A few griffins sit at the deity's feet.

In unison they pray.

After they have risen from their knees, the smallest of the boys comes and sits with me. He takes my hand. "Always the child is innocent," he says. "Never a lie on them. So God waits for him to fly into paradise and he takes him in his arms."

It is mid-morning when Sarah enters the room. "She will recover, Andronicus, but she is very weak."

I am confused. What is this? I have dozed and now I am awake again. The boys are gone, the room is cold. I struggle up. I feel my hair filled with the night before. "She—Idahlia."

"Yes, Idahlia is very weak and she will need much rest."

The silence is there, the words unspoken. Sarah speaks them after she has put her fingers on my forearm and squatted down before me. "The child is dead. I'm sorry. But in some ways it's a blessing that the child decided to come early, because had she not, your wife would have probably died as well."

For a few moments I hold my chin in my hands, my elbows resting on my knees. Sarah waits. The dawn is like a ruby, shining, and clear. And deep. I can see the camps below. Ours to the right, the military camp to the left and at the back by a motley stand of trees, the place of the courtesans.

"Would you like to see Idahlia now?"

I follow Sarah as she walks back down to the main room. The hall is dark and the candles in their sconces flicker and make odd shadows on the walls.

My wife is clean, washed. Her lips are chapped and her eyes sunken. "I have suggested that you both stay here while she recuperates. Until you are both well enough to make the journey to India."

I am all alone, back in our tent. I wanted to see it again, the damage. I want to make sure that the surplus possessions we have here go to the markets to be sold. But mostly I want to be alone with this grief. This deep pain, this hollowness.

That afternoon Sarah handed me a small bundle. She had wrapped our daughter in the green silk shawl we made for Roxane.

I dig a small grave in the back of our tent. The hole is right next to the hole that our chest lies in. I lower the small child into its bed. I pay the ferryman with some walnut shells I have filled with gold. Into each of the seven hulls I have set a small pearl. A sail of pearl, a boat of gold.

Taxila 326 BC

Taxila is serene. That is how I think of this place we have come to. The river is silver in colour and the flora is a deep, verdant green. Birds fly in and out of the branches and the plants by the riverbank are lush and plentiful. The mountains watch over us.

Idahlia is healthy again. Sarah made sure of that.

The locals peddle their wares. I am not interested and forbid Idahlia to collect anything more.

"What about those things you scratch out of the dirt like a chicken?" she says.

"They are small, Idahlia, they live in our box of good fortune. I know a gem when I see one. They cost us nothing and have brought us nothing but luck."

She sniffs. Takes more wine than she should. "It was the silk that made us."

I don't mention the tiny metal implements that I designed and help make to aid the climbers; I do not mention my father's gold which secured the white silk, and the other gems and valuables that paid for the other colours.

The day is mild. Sometimes this place is sharp in wind and wet with dew, cold with a coating of river mist. But today it is clement.

My friend is here; he wanders about most days much to the chagrin of my wife. She finds him detestable, but to me he has become a familiar voice. A man who talks with his heart. He does not wait to be asked in, rather he enters and takes the floor. I don't even know his name, so I call him the man of orange.

"I have many children," he says. He likes to practise his Greek words on us. On me. I speak slowly so he can understand. If he doesn't, he just says "repeat". I know then to phrase what I have said differently.

The village is just down the pathway that leads away from the river. His people, the people of the Rajah Abisares, live in small, whitewashed houses with coloured doors. Each door is of a different colour. For him it is orange, and he wears an orange sash.

I ask him what the orange is for.

He grins through very white teeth. "Man, it is very blessed colour. Most blessed colour of all. It is warm, is it not? It means life."

I go to ask him about the other colours of his people, like the family who wear the brown of the bark set on their white robes. But I am tired. Instead I watch as he takes the flat bread from its cotton flap and places a large piece of goat's cheese upon it.

I cannot complain, for it is Abisares who mostly feeds us. His servants deposit these rations at the top of the road each day. We have become a people who once would have rushed at it, fought over it, but in this land of complacency and calm it seems we have matured and we share it around. We ask what one might need before helping ourselves. It is only the wine that we hoard and stow away, for it has become rare. And these people of the silver river and abundant trees do not drink such a drink. Rather they take cups of soured milk sweetened with honey.

It is Sarah, not the orange man, who greets us this fine morning. The river mist has lifted and the waters below us run less swiftly. The birds are colourful and I like their chirps, their song. The flowers that hang from the trees are of deep purple and pink. Taxila is a fine place, although the orange man tells me the cold month is very cold.

"Andronicus." Sarah greets me with a hug. She has become thinner; her jawline is sharper and she wears the clothes of an Indian royal. They are quite beautiful. On her feet are slippers of gold thread. Her hair is caught under a sheer veil.

I offer her a seat and call Idahlia. She does not respond.

"How is Idahlia?" she asks.

"Well, very well. Thank you."

I pour her some wine. She holds her hand out to stop me pouring right to the top of the cup. "The Rajah's wife allows us no wine. Just juice, a little water. That is all."

I frown.

"She is something of an expert in fertility."

I do not know where to look. Sarah laughs. "I will learn much from her, but she is very fierce, Andronicus, and I am pleased to get away from their home, even it is just for a few moments."

She takes off her veil and shakes out her hair.

I excuse myself. I walk out to the small awning I have made. My wife is there, her eyes shut, but I know she is not asleep. I leave her.

"Idahlia is sleeping."

"She will feel the effects of the trauma she endured for a long time, Andronicus. The loss is terrible, her pain immense."

"I know. I know. But tell me of Roxane."

"Poor Roxane." Sarah starts laughing. "She is under a very strict regime. The Rajah's wife …" Sarah starts to demonstrate a wiping of her forehead, a sigh bigger than that of a horse. A tap of her wrist which is more of a slap. Sarah giggles, drinks more wine. "The

Rajah's wife tells Roxane and me that the Queen of Alexander has an unclean womb. Very gnarly, very dirty, must be cleaned out, if she is to conceive. For Alexander, she says, much wants a child and this is her job, to prepare the womb for the encounter with his fish."

"Tell me more," I say.

"Each morning, she is placed in a steaming bath with lots of oils and salt. Then she is taken out of it, much like you might haul a fish out of the water. She is scrubbed from head to toe with a stiff brush until even her skin is red. Then she must drink this tonic. It smells terrible. But she does it. Roxane is not one to be defeated."

It is good to see Sarah. To talk to her. Someone who I don't have to edit my speech with. Someone who seems to understand, even though we hardly know each other.

"Then, Andronicus, she is dunked in very cold water—river water. Then the servants wrap her, it does not matter if they are men, they wrap her up tight and place her in a small bed. They burn oils and chant over her."

She stops, puts her hand up and laughs again. "It's very serious I know, and I should respect such treatment of my mistress, but I cannot help but see it as a performance. Well, it is I guess. A performance. Where I come from it's the pure act of love, of someone chosen for you or by you that becomes your heart, your way to a child; a desirability of a partner that fits your needs and that is what softens the womb. The gentleness of an encounter." Her face wanders off. She is alone, single, and I wonder if she has a person of her own.

"Noon, and we are now covered in mud. Mud taken from the holy river and smoothed over her naked person. Everywhere—hair, toes—everywhere. She is placed in the sun on bricks that have been warmed. She bakes like clay in a kiln."

"Gosh." It's the only word I can come up with. I picture the beautiful Roxane, who was so kind to my wife, who was not fazed by having to roll up her sleeves and help Sarah with the birthing of a child.

"Yes, and it is the same every day. She is washed all over. Slosh, slosh, slosh with rainwater that has been stored in great barrels under the branches of the old trees that surround this home of the Rajah."

"Is it cold or hot; warm?"

"Cold, very good, nourishment from the stars, the Rajah's wife says. And then she takes a potion which puts her to sleep. She stays that way until the morning when I wake her and we begin this all over again. Oh, I forget the honey part. Her face is lathered with it as she sleeps."

"And Alexander is still not back yet?"

"No, but he is on his way. The Rajah's wife has told him he must bring his wife an elephant. For this will ensure that a child will be conceived."

"First the gift of a rock, now an elephant."

The River Jhelum 326 BC

"Yes, no good for elephants to be in battle. You see, when good man Alexander give Roxane, our beautiful lady, he tells her to watch and then he takes her away at night. I hear questions come from him," the mahout tells me, as we set up camp high on the hill above the Jhelum River.

I arch my eyebrow at him, this small, wiry, toothless man.

"Yes, it is true, Master Andronicus, very true. She answer like I tell her to. That the elephant get very frightened. She does not like shock, or fright. She does not like loud noises. She like no one coming towards her with menace. See, she will charge then back away. She has peace in her heart, this animal. But she don't like fright, noise."

This man does tasks before I even instruct him to. At the moment he is weaving baskets from the tall grasses that grow on this site. "Good to store food in baskets, hang them from the good banyan trees. Good tree to make our fires beneath."

I'm weary. Each journey brings more fatigue. If I'd had the choice to stay in Taxila, I may well have done so. I liked the people, the place, the food, the loveliness.

I stand and watch my party arrive. Roxane has been carried in a litter. She is dressed in her Indian clothes. Sarah walks beside her, lean and strong. My wife I put her in one of our carts and had one of our allotted guards hitch a horse to it and carry her here.

The soldiers have come before us and have set up camp on this bank of the Jhelum River.

I see with my own eyes—our foe. A mass of men. A camp that runs at least six deep. Their horses are plump, ours are scrawny. Their men hold their weapons erect. We are fewer in number. We have no elephants in our rank. We do not know the terrain so well. I think this will be our end.

And as instructed by the King himself, I build our home high on this bank. He tells me that she, his wife, must be protected from all things, and the monsoon is expected soon. So I, with the help of the mahout and the appointed guards, dig channels in the soil so that rain will run past us. I instruct them to build floors, raised beds so that damp—water of any kind—will not touch those who sleep. The mahout has already hoisted food high up in those trees captured in a basket weave so fine that neither bird, nor rodent, nor bat will gorge themselves on the food we have either collected or been given.

"And master, most important –" The mahout stands before me, his feet unable to stay still, "– most important, five fires must be kept alight. For this is the way to enlightenment, this is the way in which all souls are kept in the heart of the world."

Each day I sit on the bank and look at the lines of men below. At dawn the troops line up, Poros on the other side of the river, our men on this side, facing each other. Prepared. Waiting for a signal. No one side wanting to make the first move.

Every day Craterus looks as if he will give the signal to ford the river and attack, then at the last minute he changes his mind. "As you were," he calls to his men.

"It is deliberate." Roxane says as she sits like me, watching.

"We have fewer men; it makes sense to wait and hope that Poros will capitulate." We both stare at the large numbers of men Poros has lined up, the elephants, the horses, their tall spears, their light garments.

"They aim to frustrate the Rajah; they do this with intent."

"What?"

"Yes, it is tiring for us to watch this charade, day after day, but it more tiring for the enemy."

"For our side too."

"In some ways, but in some ways not. You see, Alexander and Craterus ensure that their men are well fed on fish and wine at the end of each day. They have tents to shelter them, and courtesans to please them. But Poros, he has not based a camp here. The men sit on the ground, some even wander home, then regroup the next day."

I rise and dust off my chiton; the clouds are heavy.

"Look upstream," Roxane says.

I hold my hand over my eyes and study the soldiers that line our side of the bank.

"Can you see?"

"What am I looking at?"

"The line of soldiers, Andronicus. When they first assembled here on the very first day of the campaign, Craterus' last line of soldiers was in line with our banyan trees. Now this last line is stationed further upstream."

"So they have moved."

"Each day a little further north. Hardly noticeable."

I leave her. I feel tired. This heat, this thick air, the insects that have begun to gather in swarms. Great armies of them.

We are sitting down around the fires under the banyan trees. They remind me of old men, these trees with their knotty faces and rugged arms. Tonight the mahout serves us not fish, but a stew made from the bitter herbs that grow down in the valley over the hill. He has placed in it a sauce made from wild mushrooms, and on top he has sprinkled chopped walnuts and some of his special dried fish rations. On the side he's placed two boiled eggs taken from a nest on the riverbank.

We eat in silence.

"The rain, just like I told you, master, will come soon. Big rain. Monsoon. And it is good, master, that we build the camp here. On this hill, under the trees with our fire and food. And you will see our elephant will come to us when the rains come. Now she prefers the valley in her little hut that I made her, but when the rains arrive she will come to protect us and give us strength."

The man of orange briefed me on the monsoon too—a blessing to be endured, for it gives life.

And of course Alexander chose the site on which we would camp. High above, so that when his son is born he will see the glorious victory of his father.

On the advice of the mahout and the man of orange I built raised platforms with pole legs; I dug channels and lined the sides with rock.

Roxane is small in size; her protrusion is flat across her belly. Yet each day she pats it and tells Sarah that she is fine. She tells all of us not to fuss, that she's fine.

Aristander has read the omens. The left lobe of the slice of dog's liver in the auspicious ritual was more coloured than the right, and therefore a son would be born. Alexander's heir—the heir to the world.

The Syrian seer, Fida, was nowhere to be seen. When I enquired about her, General Ptolemy told me she had fallen to her death at the top of the world.

———

117

Idahlia spends much of her day sleeping. We were asked by Alexander in Taxila if we would be the custodians, the guardians of his expectant wife, and when the child was born that we would be his aides. It was a honour to be asked. But Idahlia's eyes did not brighten at this royal directive.

Alexander, with Craterus by his side, had walked out to our small tent and we had invited them in. I poured them wine and it was then that he announced that his wife had conceived. The Rajah's wife was certain that inside her womb a flower bloomed; that the elephant had brought blessings to the royal crown and that under the capable care of a woman who knows about the stars and the moon and all the Gods that gather to create a child, she had played her part.

Idahlia sat on one of our plainer cushions, staring at the carpet. She traced the birds and the deer, the trees, and then a curious smile sat on her lips.

Craterus noticed her disposition. He put his arm out and gave her a coin from his pocket. "A very old coin that I found near the banks of the river," he said. She took it and did not look at it. She placed it under our rug like a small child.

"Did you see the crocodiles at the river too?" she asked.

"Gharials—they look very much like crocodiles, but they are in fact gharials. They eat fish, not men."

"And the grasses, like the grains found on the Nile, I am told."

"Yes, you could say they are similar, but of course the Egyptians have a whole industry based on grains, all kinds of grains. The biggest granaries in all the world."

"We march down this riverbank as far as the river runs and then we reach Egypt. I very much want to live in Egypt," Idahlia said.

Alexander had stopped talking to me and had started to listen to my wife. Craterus stood, and asked if perhaps we might all have some more wine.

"Yes, yes, of course," I said, and filled all our cups. Idahlia held hers out, waiting until I returned to fill hers up to the brim.

"Idahlia—it is Idahlia, isn't it?" Craterus began. "We are far from Egypt, we have yet to cross the four rivers of India. It will be a good thing to do, to establish what really lies beyond this land of ours now."

Idahlia held her hands to her ears. I walked to her, as fast as I could, pulled her hands from her face and held them tight. "Yes, it will be, and a privilege for us to be in the camp of Roxane. To help her in this next stage of producing the heir."

That was then and this is now.

The sleeping Idahlia, the listless and fatigued Idahlia. The much-changed Idahlia. I stroke her moist forehead as she lies on our spacious bed, high upon this riverbank, overlooking soldiers about to do battle, and wonder if, when she was so ill in Sogdia, a part of her did not heal. If when she lost the baby in Bactria, something else in her died too.

As I walk outside, I notice the clouds that have fallen in low in the sky. They are grey, verging on black. One single raindrop hits me on my cheek. Then another; they are heavy raindrops. Large and full. Then it comes in sheets. The ground throws up dirt as the drops fall.

A great rumble of thunder startles us. The mahout is outside in only a loin cloth, jumping up and down and lifting his eyes to the sky, allowing the rain to wash his face. "Do not fear, it is the monsoon. It has arrived."

A lightning bolt pierces the darkness. Zeus' weapon throws flames of white into this Indian sky. And down below I see them move.

Alexander's men must have forded the river upstream. They must have surrounded Poros' army on the other side. A semi-circle of our men firing arrows into the centre of Poros' lines.

Craterus' men then ford the river in front of us. They attack head on.

We won the battle against Poros just days ago, it seems, but the rain is now the enemy. The soldiers below us shiver under their worn blankets, they try to keep their fires alight. The river is swift and the water rises to the bank. There is no fishing at such a time. And then it is the bugs; ugly little monsters that fly and whizz at us. That bite and sting us. From the sodden soil that is nothing but a mud lake comes even more creatures.

All we can do in our camp is sit under the trees and sip warm wine. Sarah is concerned for Roxane, for the flying insects have eaten her and left her swollen with bites. The Queen, our lady, does not complain, she simply sloshes them with salt and jokes with the mahout about how she has turned into some sort of monster.

The mahout says, "The elephant appear soon and heal you."

As the weapons rust below, the tents mould up and become useless, and the soldiers starve, eating only what the ground throws up. Roxane's bites become worse. In this humid air, they turn yellow with pus. Roxane refuses to take to her bed, so Sarah administers some of her black paste. She protests but finally the mother-to-be sleeps inside our less-wet tents.

The mahout pleads with us to be patient. To allow the water to do its job.

Idahlia cries. She weeps. And I can bring her no comfort except the warm wine which, like the black paste, sends her into a kind stupor. I lie beside her, hearing the banging of the monsoon on the tent. It is not an unpleasant sound, made less so, I guess, by the fact that we were prepared. We painted our tent's exterior with beeswax and animal fat. The man of orange told me this. We dug small canals so the water could run past us.

And just as it started, quickly, without delay, the monsoon is over. A bright sun, hot, comes into the sky and starts to dry up the earth. Great tiles of mud create cracks in which bright flowers sprout up. The oranges and yellows, the pinks and reds; these blooms colour the world beneath our feet.

We see clearly the tidy up below. The rallying of the men. The attendance of Poros' people who place offerings at the place where Alexander pours out libations to the Gods each day.

There is talk of moving. And we see the preparation begin. Yes, now Alexander and his men will walk across India.

"His ranks have diminished," Sarah says.

I say nothing. That tiredness is set so hard inside me that my mind refuses to move.

"Many died, Andronicus, of fever. Some drowned, some were already ill from previous battle wounds and the air here opened them out and let the poison in."

It is a sad sight, this army. Victorious, with the only Rajah to oppose Greek rule, now made the Satrap of his own former region. The Greek uniforms are threadbare, the weapons not polished and shining. The carts made heavy by water.

"Coenus, an old general who served under Phillip, is urging Alexander to turn back now, before they all die en route," Sarah says.

Back home we made knives and swords and spears for General Coenus. His symbol is the bull. I remember making such a symbol, etching it on the handle of a dagger.

When General Craterus calls before they leave, it is Sarah who walks forth and greets him. I see them talking, discussing. She seems to be pleading with him. I should join them, listen, give my support, my thoughts.

I approach, and Sarah turns to me. "She must stay put. She is still not well. Those bites still fester and I fear for the child."

"Yes, she was bitten." It is all I can manage.

Craterus strokes his chin. "Should she not have birthed by now?"

"No, no, Craterus, she is still a moon cycle away."

"We had hoped to take the heir to paradise, so that his small feet might touch the golden sands."

"I know," Sarah says, "but I think any travel now will endanger not only her but also the unborn child."

"Well then, we can't have that. She will stay here in relative comfort. I will have the new Satrap Poros supply you with whatever you may need. She will birth here and then you will bring both baby and child to meet us."

"Thank you," Sarah says, the sweat dripping from her face. She wipes it away with her hands. "Thank you, Craterus."

"And you agree with this, Andronicus?"

"Yes. Yes." I say.

The mahout disappears with the elephant, we know not where. We miss him. I miss him. And as I take his nets and place them in the river, I feel a sense of foreboding. I dismiss it as silly superstition. My father hated such stuff. My mother, however, believed in many such signs given in warning. If a black moth settled nearby, someone close would die. If a black cat crossed the path in front of you, it was a sign of good luck. If a pig fell ill and died on the road to market, a plague was on its way.

I pull up the full nets. *Fish—feed her mashed-up fish, with a little river water and she will heal.* That is what the mahout told me.

I fry the fish. I cannot bear to mash them. I yell to Sarah to come and eat. But she shouts back to me, her head poking out the tent door. "She is cramping."

I say fish, give her fish. Sarah shouts at me again. "No, Andronicus, no, she is in labour, we need hot water, linens, I need to sluice my instruments in salt water and strong wine. As Idahlia is indisposed at present, it is you who must help me."

I shake as I rub Sarah's fine scissors dry and lay out the linen under our lady. As I place wet cloths over her brow; honey on her lips. As I place just a dot of the black poppy paste on her tongue.

Roxane groans, a most unholy groan. Animal like. The grunts continue and it is then that I see the moth. A black moth on the white wall of the tent.

"Foolish." I say.

"Sorry …" Sarah says.

"It is nothing."

Sarah is sitting on a stool, her hands near the opening of the vagina. Every so often she goes to Roxane's stomach and pushes hard on it. "That's it … good, you are doing fine."

Apart from the groans and grunts, Roxane has said nothing. But then, as we begin to ease into the task of getting this baby free from the womb, Roxane rises. "I must walk. I must walk outside."

———

So we follow her as she heads towards the banyan trees. She pushes against their trunks, moving down the stand of five. Each tree she hugs and presses her face into the bark. She leans and lets the trees hold her.

Sarah stands back. "What can I do?" she says.

I'm just pleased that we are away from the moth. I watch as finally Roxane lets out a cry. Sarah rushes forward, but Roxane has already caught her baby. It dangles with its cord.

"Cut the cord," she yells at Sarah.

Roxane holds the baby. It makes no sound. "He's beautiful," she says.

Sarah moves to take the child, but Roxane pushes her away. "Quite perfect, no lie upon his tongue. He will be taken without judgment into the kingdom of heaven.

We witness the tears fall on the newborn's face, clear and crystal-like. Roxane makes no noise as she cries. Her face does not puff up with her weeping. She rocks the dead child and shows him the river, the trees, the mountains up to the north. "And across there your Daddy will touch the sea," she tells him.

The moon has turned full again and I sit with Sarah. Both Idahlia and Roxane sleep. We think the same thought. How it happened, we do not know. Why it happened, I understand. We blame ourselves. Sarah and I berate ourselves, not each other; instead we make excuses for one another.

"It was my job, Andronicus, to watch the child."

"No, I was appointed custodian, guardian of this camp, it was totally my doing."

We send word via one of Poros' men to the camp of Alexander, that the heir was born, but without breath.

Then this Indian man, this beautiful Indian man, Poros himself, arrives at our camp. He brings gifts of gold and gems and incense. He sits cross-legged before our fire. He puts out his hands to warm himself. "He has turned back. Alexander has turned back."

He takes our wine, smiles and declares that it is delicious.

"Why is he turning back?" Sarah says.

"There were some disagreements. His men, they are tired. They have travelled further than any other men in the world. Their bodies are hurting. General Coenus led a revolt and our gracious King had no option but to listen to this learned man, a great friend of his father's, because his own men took the side of the old General, not the side of our beloved. So they now turn back."

It isn't long before we hear the clatter of horses' hooves, the banging of drums and the chatter of men. Sarah says she will go alone to explain to Alexander what happened.

"No we will go together."

We wait outside the King's tent. It is very hot and we did not bring water or wine with us. We hear shouts and protests from inside the planning room. Finally, we are granted an audience.

The air inside is stale and stinks of sweat and unwashed bodies. The King's hair is knotted and tangled. Hephaestion is asleep one corner. Craterus is not there. Ptolemy takes the lead.

"So, we are very disappointed in you, Sarah. This was your one and only job, to bring that child safely into the world." Ptolemy says.

Alexander holds his head in his hands, he scribbles on parchment.

I ache for her now. Sarah stands. She is tall, erect and willing to take whatever punishment is given to her.

"But it is not only this, is it, Sarah –" he pauses, "– that has made us disappointed in you. That makes us regret your appointment to be the girl's handmaiden and midwife."

"Yes, yes. I had no hand in what happened to the child. In my opinion the baby died while still the womb. That happens. But I did do wrong when it came to not guarding his corpse."

Alexander bangs his hand. "You allowed the child to be fed to the wild animals. To be left on a hill, in the cold of night, to be nothing but bones in the morning."

"Yes, I apologise and regret it very much. If I could go back in time, I would. I would have swaddled him and had him brought to you."

I try to speak, but Ptolemy pushes me back down in my seat.

"And again, Sarah, we hear that the blood of two infants is on your hands. We hear from our sources that whilst in our employ you did deliver another baby. Another dead baby."

My heart drops. Something disappears from my field of vision.

"Did or did she not, Andronicus, pass a dead baby over to you after you wife's delivery."

"Yes, but …"

"Did Sarah kill your child?"

"No, the child—"

"Was your baby dead after being in the hands of this midwife here?"

I cannot answer. I will not answer. Ptolemy pokes me in the ribs.

"Our child died. But—"

"Sarah, you are to be spared. Oh, some of us would like you to hang, but Alexander has asked that you be spared. You will go home to Bactria and resume your duties at the Court of Artabazus. A guide waits for you."

Ptolemy turns to me. "Andronicus, send the girl to us now."

The Mourning Tent 326 BC

Roxane stands before her husband. It is dark and the little silver bugs with the silver wings, the harmless ones, begin their chorus. She has listened to them often. The humming, the strumming of night music.

She feels numb; she feels nothing, but she hears every little sound that is about her. The drumming of her husband's fingers on the dusty table. Hephaestion sipping his cup. Ptolemy pacing up and down.

It is the silence that is unbearable. She stretches her ears even further to hear the soft roll of the river.

"Well, what do you have to say?" Ptolemy asks.

"He was born perfect. He has been taken up to the kingdom above. No lie has soiled his tongue, no sin has entered his body."

"You fed him to the birds!" Alexander stands up and comes to her. He is very near now, so very near. She smells the wine on his breath. She smells his odour.

She would like to move back.

"So for your sin, if that is what you want to call it," Ptolemy says, "you will be sent to the tent of mourning. You will learn from the masters how one prepares a body. You will learn how the deceased is to be honoured in death."

"Here's the Barbarian girl," one of the guards says as she arrives at the tent, which is a fair way from any of the other camps. The occupants, gathered around a raised table, laugh.

Large bunches of leaves hang off suspended ropes; the floor is just grass, the people are dressed in red. All in red. And they all look similar. All of one family.

"Don't just stand there," a woman yells at her. "Here, come, put this on." She hands her a red apron. She fumbles with the ties as she secures them around her thin body. The apron is very large; these people are very large. "We have saved the best jobs for you; apparently those were the King's orders." Again the cackle, the laugh, as if this man before them, dead on a table, is not there at all.

The smell, the heat; she has to hold in the vomit that rises in her throat. She proceeds towards the table, the bier, as it is called. The woman who handed her the apron now passes her some rags. "So now plug up his rear end, and to do that you need to lift up that side of his rump and stuff them in. Make sure you use all of them; we don't want him leaking."

As she does this, a small boy combs the hair of the fallen general. Coenus. She knows him only by sight. He is black and blue, his skin torn in places. Blood has dried on his upper lip.

The lady speaks again to her directly. "Funny, isn't it, that the man who persuaded his lordship to return to the west, to our homelands, is now dead before us. Now be a good love and wipe that blood from his lips."

Roxane finds a clean linen and dips it in a bucket of dirty river water. She cleans up this old man's lips. She is gentle. As gentle as she can be. The little boy smiles at her. He is perched on a stool.

"Now see that thread there? Stitch up his mouth."

Roxane does as this woman commands. The needle is blunt and she struggles to sew it together. The woman takes over. "Give it here." And within a few moments the lips are sewn tight. They look awful. It is as if the woman reads her thoughts.

"Don't worry, love. By the time we finish with him he will look as good as new."

They paint his face with mud tinted with colour. They paint his lips, they run kohl around his eyes. They dress him in a set of clean military clothes. They even put sandals on his feet. The little boy cleans out the dirt from under his toenails. They dress the bier in foliage.

"Time to party," the woman shrieks. "Pay day, love."

She is dragged to another part of the tent and behind the screen they remove their red clothes and don long capes of black. The woman takes Roxane's hair and pins clumps of hair into it with metal clips. "You see, you pull them, love, when we march. You tear out your hair and leave it on the ground, and you, little Hector, don't you forget, love, to collect them bits of hair after we have marched away."

They wait until the horn is sounded. Then, as solemn as her father was when it came to special rituals, they set off. The older boys carry the bier upon their shoulders. They walk past a line of assembled soldiers. Then the old woman starts to sing. It is a joyless song.

When they reach the river, another member of this family, a man worn by time, greets the procession, clutching a stick. As Roxane walks past to take her position at the back of the official mourners, he pulls her aside.

"The King has asked this of you." He places two gold coins in her palm. His hand is covered in veins, raised and blue. He bends down to her so that his instructions come as a whisper. "Listen," he says. "You will climb the ladder up to the top of pyre where old Coenus will be placed." He stops. "Understand?"

She nods.

"Then you will place the coins on his eyelids."
She begins to move forward but he pulls her back. "You
will be called by your husband when the time is right. He
will throw the flare into the dry wood stack, once you
have paid the ferryman."

The Indus 325 BC

Idahlia and Andronicus are her only companions. There are two guards, one stationed at the very back and one stationed a little ahead. But they are not part of their party. For her wrong doings she has been positioned at the rear of Craterus' line; at the very back, the very end. Ahead are the civilians, the courtesans, and the soldiers.

"Even the measly herds that some civvies have gathered up walk ahead of us," Idahlia says.

Andronicus does not say much, but he is always considerate in his conduct. Idahlia speaks more and more each day as they walk, for she believes it is this road that will take them to Egypt.

Andronicus speculates that they will march down the Indus and at some point turn inland to walk over Persia and return to Greece.

When they camp, it is awkward. Andronicus sits carving wood, polishing up a stone, spooning out the few edibles he has found on their journey. They are given wine. When it arrives, often Andronicus will trade it for fresh meat or fish. And Idahlia complains about this.

"Stuck here," Idahlia says to her, this night when all the stars are out and the moon is nearly full. "Stuck here but soon to be in Egypt, and my friends the courtesans do tell me I will be free there. To find a house, to fill our stores."

Andronicus looks to his wife with concern. She has not mingled with the courtesans since she washed for them.

When Idahlia is in bed and they hear her snoring, meaning she is fast asleep, Andronicus sits beside her, flicking bits of dried grass into his fire, watching as the thin reeds dwindle. "She believes many strange things, Roxane. Forgive her, she seems to have sunk into a place where I cannot reach her."

Roxane nods. "The place is called madness. That's how we speak of it at home."

"And what do your people do with madness?"

"Muni is the keeper of the potions, the keeper of all things that heal. Sometimes she uses the wort to make a tea but when the madness starts to erode the self or the other selves, she will use something stronger to calm the person with the madness."

"What do you mean, *hurt the self, or other selves*?"

"Some start to pierce themselves and slice their skin." Roxane remembers a time when an old man did this. He watched his blood flow and said he was letting out the bad spirits. She had had to hold spider webbing on his wounds until the blood clotted.

"Oh well, at least Idahlia doesn't hurt herself, or others."

Roxane nods.

"But her words do sting these days." He winks at her and pours them more wine. They watch the sky on this clear night. The river is tranquil as it takes its life out into the sea.

She finds it hard to sleep. She sits out often in the candlelight, preferring the freshness of the outdoors to the stuffiness of their small tent. She collects stones and builds small houses with them.

This day, much like any other, begins with the pack-up and the wait as the line starts to move forward. But then at midday they come to an abrupt stop.

"Halt!" Men of rank run up and down the banks issuing orders. "No further! Stop!"

"Need to rest anyway," Idahlia says. She slumps down on the banks of the river and places her swollen ankles into a deep pool.

"Come, come." She pats the ground beside her. But Roxane does not sink her hot feet into the cool water, for it's not right to place what is not meant to be in water. Water is life, the very thing that needs to be pure in order that our blood runs clean. Roxane watches each day how the Greeks and their followers tip out their slops into the Indus. How they spit into it. She has even seen one soldier defecate straight into the river.

She instead sits and lies back against a solitary tree. The shade is welcome. These days her dresses are worn, her feet bare. But she finds this life not so bad. She is left alone and that is some kind of peace.

Suddenly she is aware of a change. All around her people have become agitated. Their voices are high and shrill. She sees men fall down on their knees and cry. She sees others start to loot the campsites of others.

Andronicus looks down the river, shades his brow with his hand and then looks back to his wife and Roxane. "I will go and find out what has happened."

It is not long before he is back, red cheeked and out of breath. "There was an attack. Unexpected."

"What happened?" Roxane says.

"Alexander decided to call on a small tribe, the Malli, quite some distance from here. But when he walked into their surrounds they attacked him. So he counterattacked, throwing himself over their walls and in doing so a spear was driven into his side." Andronicus looks grim. "They fear he will die."

"Oh, the silly man. Can't he just leave well alone? We are rich and we are nobles now. We do not need such trouble," Idahlia says.

A lone Indian man in a loin cloth comes running down the bank. "He is truly a god! He rose from the dead. It was predicted he wouldn't last the night but early, before the light, he had a white horse brought to his boat on the river and he mounted it and rode amongst the elite."

She makes mental notes of the colour that the river shows them. One day grey, the next a darker green and some days the brown runs wild down its rocks. The river has moods; sad, happy, remorseful. She drinks in its splendour. The river; the happiness of the river. Her estranged husband lives. Their walk will continue.

The dusk is nearly over; the silhouetted outlines of those trees on the bank across the river take their turn to be admired. Roxane regards Idahlia. The first time she met her she was in labour, in agony. Her hair long was in a plait down her back. She had no grey in her hair then, she does now. Her face is lined and rutted.

Andronicus has a strong build, a quiet, confident voice. But now he is hunched a little. His skin is wrinkled and leathery. The road has changed them all. The journey has made them a little less resilient. Each time something unfavourable happens, a little more becomes broken.

Roxane examines her hands. They are cracked and dry, like when she worked in the field. But her nails are not smooth, her skin is not scented. When she worked in the Sogdian fields, at least at the end of each day she would sit with her mother and Muni and they would rub their nails smooth with little silver graters, and they would rub oil into their hands. Often Muni would wrap them in cotton so that in the morning when they peeled off the layers, their hands would look new.

She wonders, what will happen? She will live as an outcast. But she smiles up at the few stars that light the heavens tonight. In her heart she knows she has not betrayed her God, or her own people. She has maintained and stayed true to the words of the prophet. Zarathustra. The prophet who taught them that the most important thing was to feed, shelter and keep warm your people. The second is never to lie. The third is never to soil the nest in which you live.

She talks to the river again, her silent voice radiates out over the pools, pools that have darkened to blue. *To be here, is not to be there. To be here is to live alone. And for that I am grateful. For if that never changes, if I am to be settled in a corner of the outside of this new realm, I am grateful that I will not be bothered by anyone. I can talk to the waters, to the sky, to Mother Moon. I will let my face be warmed by the beacon of my God.*

She moves so her feet make no noise. She loves this practice, this game. Oxyartes would make her compete with the other children and she always won. The quiet walker. If she was left alone without anyone she could hunt for food. She would maybe walk back north and across India to the coast. And she would stand where Alexander did not stand. She would see if indeed there was another paradise. A paradise on earth.

She doesn't hear him. As she settles beneath her tree she sees him in the darkness near her spot. He is sitting watching the river.

"It is elegant tonight." He turns to her and says, "Isn't the deep blue of the water very different tonight?"

"Yes, it is. I do not know why, for there are not so many stars and Mother Moon's belly is not full," Roxane says to General Craterus, who is chewing on a stalk of grass.

"This is a good spot."

"Yes, always a tree. If Andronicus stops in a barren place, I ask that we might move further back a little, or forward, so that at least we have the benefit of a tree.”

"Not a tent but a tree.”

"Yes.”

Craterus takes her hand and tells her to look deep into the water in front of them. "You pitched your camp on an excellent site tonight, for it's rare, what appears in the water tonight.”

She peers deep into its dark well. She sees circles, many circles, perfect circles that spread in and out. Then she sees a sleek white form. A fish. A long nose.

"They are the white dolphins of the Indus. They are rare.”

She has heard of dolphins, the tame and gentle sea creatures that have been known to save men from drowning. Phaidros told her of them. She walks nearer to the edge and watches as a head comes out of the water. The long mouth seems to smile at her.

"It's a good omen. They bring luck. Few people ever get to see them.”

As they sit and watch them vanish, Craterus speaks. "There is a plan,” he begins. "I come this night so that we are left to speak alone. So that nobody will hear. I have checked on all those around and they sleep soundly in their beds.” He pauses. She waits. "So most of us will be ordered to walk to the sea and then to follow the coastline around until we reach Persia. They will regroup at Salmous. Alexander takes this route, for he desires to walk in the footsteps of Heracles. However, many of the men, the veterans among us, are not strong enough to make this journey. The coastline is a journey, a battle. It's hard on foot as the walkers must climb over sharp rocks. They must endure the heat of that place.”

"I can endure heat. I am used to the Sogdian summer and I am used to rocks.”

"Yes, but you see, Roxane, you are not going around the sea route. You are to be part of my party. I will come for you in a few nights' time. You must tell no one of these plans."

She's dozing when she feels the tap on her shoulder. Craterus puts his finger to his lips and they sneak up around the side of tent in which Idahlia and Andronicus sleep and up past the sleeping guard in his small bivvy.

They run, soft footed, until they are well clear of the line. "My men, the old vets have already been marched off to the west. They are camped a little way from here, but first I must prepare you."

Roxane says nothing. He takes a bag from his shoulder and places it on the ground. He widens the drawstrings at its neck and takes out some garments. He shows her the bushes at the right and asks her please to wear the clothes he has laid out for her.

Roxane stops. "Please, you could just let me go. I will be fine. I will wander north-east and you will never hear from me again. I will not go back to Sogdia. I will remain a solitary person until the day I die."

Craterus takes her by the shoulders. "You are valuable to the Macedonian crown, you are the one we need."

"But I have done such wrong in the eyes of your people."

"You birthed a dead child. It happens. And Alexander still needs an heir."

"But it should not be by me."

"It will be you."

"He could take more wives; he could take a more royal woman. There are many, and much more suitable than me."

"He wants you; Roxane you are everything he looks for in a person. Beautiful, strong, level-headed, intelligent. You speak our language as if it is your own."

Roxane starts to walk away, but he pulls her back with a firm grip. "We have a plan. It's vital that you play your part."

"What part?"

"I will tell you once you go and put on your new clothes."

She returns dressed as a young boy. In clothes that a page might wear. Baggy pants and a long chiton. Her garb is a mixture of Persian and Greek. The chiton is embroidered with birds, the breeches a crimson colour.

"So you are now Jasper, my new houseboy and servant to Nico, my man-servant."

"Where is Roxane, where has she gone?"

"Oh, she has been inserted somewhere in the coastal line. She is no longer the charge of the good Andronicus and his sharp-tongued wife."

"Where in the line, with whom?"

"That is a secret, a very unspecific place, neither here nor there." Craterus takes a small knife, in shape of snake, from his breast pocket. He rubs his finger along its curled blade to make sure it is sharp and then he takes her hair and begins to cut it so it sits upon her shoulders. "One last thing, you do not need to speak much, you speak Greek well because your father from the southern court attached to Darius in Babylon taught you well. Nico my manservant knows of your true self, but no one else except Alexander and Hephaestion."

Overland 325 BC

The position is not arduous. She rides with Craterus over the land of golden sands. The light on most days is magnificent. She sleeps at his feet in the tent and Nico sleeps in the next room. She is fed well and Nico mutters to her about everything: how the gardens in Pella at this time of year are to die for; how his mother made a stew similar to the one they enjoyed tonight. "You know he has the best cooks. That is what he chooses first, not the men and how competent they are in battle, but the cooks. For a good soldier need fine food in his belly."

Roxane notices how Craterus sets his camp up in lines, with a small gap every now and then. How another tent is erected there which Nico tells her is the mess tent. They stop in the late afternoon. "This," says Nico, "is the time for rest and relaxation."

"The old veterans are well pleased," Nico says. "Pleased, my dear Jasper, for they are going home. All they have longed for since Persepolis. They are fed, and dear Craterus does not push them too hard."

This night is warm and they have dined on a pig that the scouts up ahead found in an abandoned field with an apple tree right in its centre. Craterus asks Jasper to walk with him. They leave Nico straightening the tent, tidying and folding and making up beds. They sit on the hillside away from guards and away from the camp.

As he pointed out the Indus dolphins to her, Craterus now points to a parade of little lights journeying below. "Arabian traders. They walk by night and sleep, hidden, in the day."

He takes her down but not to the lights, just down the slope far enough out of sight from any prying eyes. And then he kisses her. He undresses her.

"Craterus, no. The lie of who I am is enough. Not this."

"It's part of the plan Jasper."

They ride the next day. And the next. Each night it is the same. Craterus spirits Jasper away somewhere out of sight, and they lie together. They rise before the light and resume their roles.

In her heart she does not mind it. She does not dislike this man. Always she has felt somehow drawn to him. The nights with Alexander, in Taxila, were rushed and tense. He never really held her, or kissed her on the lips. But Craterus makes her body come alive. She longs for it, for the act, during the day as they ride. Each night he pleases her, and she experiences this gift of love.

When they are a day's ride from Salmous, Craterus takes a meeting with a scout. He comes for her once he has dismissed the scout and calls for Nico to join them. They sit in his well-appointed lounge. "I have had varied reports of the excursion around the coasts of the south," says Craterus. "A tragic tale of death and a very arduous course. I did wonder, as you know, my dear Nico, what my friend—our friend—was thinking when he proposed taking this route. He had many warnings of course, but Alexander is Alexander."

"Alexander is stubborn," Nico says.

"The good news is that he lives. Ptolemy lives. Hephaestion lives. Many did make it across this treacherous land, but many perished too."

Craterus stands. He paces. "Now this is how it will go. Jasper is no longer, Nico, he has come down with a terrible fever and you must bury him out in the sands there."

Roxane feels the blunt force of death upon her. "No, not bury, don't bury me, leave me exposed. Leave me, walk on ahead and leave me. Really. I am ready for death."

"But Roxane lives," Craterus says.

"She does," Nico says. He stands and moves to a chest from which he takes out her old, battered gown.

"This is what you must do." Craterus stops and stares at her. "You will dress tonight in this attire. Nico will bury the clothes of Jasper as his body. But Roxane did not die at all, she marched over the mighty Makran and survived that fiery land. You will walk to Salmous tomorrow just before dawn and take up residence in a shelter that has been put aside for you."

"How will I know where to go?"

"I have a Salmousian man coming for you. He is the one whose hut you will stay in. It has all been arranged. He speaks not a word of Greek. Alexander knows of your miraculous survival, and this is why he has given you a home in which to recover and regain your strength. He did visit you several times on the journey and even more recently, and is praying for an heir."

She does not say it. She thinks it. The lie, the deception. But what did her father say when he was going to tell Alexander and his men that Shapur had died of a fever?

A lie told to protect what little life is left is a lie that God will understand. The little life that might lie in her.

Salmous 325 BC

I'm in the Shades, the dark place. I am dead. Above is a domed roof of the darkest brown. Out of the corner of my eye I can just grasp a shape of green; a leaf waving up and down. There is a mumbling.

I sink back down into sleep. Sleep.

My head aches. It is a vice. My eyes hurt. And my mouth is as dry as dry.

"He's awake." There is a voice. I know the voice; perhaps I know the voice. I don't know.

A wanderer from the Shades is beside me. His in white robes and has no teeth. Then that voice with a face comes over me. I know her. She wipes my brow and rubs something sweet on my lips.

"Andronicus." She makes me take water from a damp cloth. "Suck on it."

"Where?" The light coming in from the arched way is bright. I squint. The wanderer moves like a beggar man and he places a curtain over the hole. Then there is the waving of green leaves, to and fro, and a breeze comes over my face. I am moving from life to death, to death, to death.

When I wake I can see. The throbbing in my head is gone. I lift myself up on my elbow and it is Roxane that comes to me. "You survived," I say to her. "How did you find me?" I am so happy, so pleased to see her that I start to weep.

The man, the wanderer is behind me now, placing cushions at the back of my shoulders so I can rest my back on the dark wall. It is cool there; the wall is very cool.

She kneels beside me and I take her hand. "You were in front. Yes, a better place to be. Many died, some in arms, the desert, some just washed away in the waters."

"You must eat something, Andronicus. Here, I have some thick fermented milk. It will help your stomach."

She feeds me with a silver spoon. She smells of the earth.

"Where is this place?"

"Salmous. And this good man here gave me the loan of his hut. It is beautiful. All made of pressed and polished mud."

"And how …?"

"I found you, Andronicus, in a field not far from this door. You would not wake but you had breath in you."

When I have finished the bowl of yoghurt, she says I must sleep. I feel my lids heavy again and sink back down into that floor of mud.

This day I will remember, for I am better and stronger, and I can sit up now for long periods of time. I can feel my legs and my arms. The old man, the house-owner, sits chewing something. He has a strong smell but it does not worry me. It is a smell that suits this home of his. He waves the branch with the leaves and they make patterns on his wall. Muted patterns, much like that of a woven basket.

It started in the harbour. I remember that. The harbour we were so excited to see. Boats and blue sea, big waves and there was a lagoon. That is where we camped the night. We feasted on oysters and wine and some of that beer that the locals like. Idahlia was so happy. She was going to her new place. She sang that night, and all those around her joined in. The lights, the boats in the harbour. Everything so merry. Alexander had told us we would just follow the shore. The sea was on the left of us and the shore on the right. It was an easy map, he said. He had commandeered the boats from the local fisherman. They were stocked with all the victuals we would need: fresh water, salted fish, dates, olives, oils, wine.

What happened next? I rack my brain to find the memory. It was fine, yes, three days of bliss. Walking a coastline; bathing our feet in the waves on the shores. The boats sailed with us a little way out and then the men would row ashore in smaller boats with the food we would eat that evening.

I lie down. I need to close my eyes. To remember. And that is it … the day it all went wrong. We turned into a bay that was set further inland; we needed to walk inland to reach the next port. And there they were. Creatures crawling like monsters on the stony beach. We smelt them before we saw them. As we drew closer, we saw that they were in fact people. Stout people with long hair threaded with seaweed, who wore coats of fish skin. The ran at us, howled at us, guarded their pots of sea bones and fish heads.

We retreated inland, for there was no next bay. This wretched bay of the sea people turned into a sheer cliff. So on Alexander's instructions we moved inland. We would hunt for food; find nourishment in the springs and the plants that we would surely come across.

We were still joyful. There was wine and we had water. We came after two days to a green pasture. And the military said they would take the upper region while the civilians would take the lower, softer, grassy region.

We ate good food. Roasted bird. Fried water greens. And then Idahlia and I lay in our tent. We felt good. We held each other. She spoke of new children. She told me of her dream, a house of white, with a room in which she would sew. She said that in Egypt there were many fabrics. Linens, silks, cottons. That the Egyptian woman cut a good cloth. The men too. And she would be again the one they would turn to in order to be the best dressed.

The rain came. At first it was a little rain, but then it poured. The rain came up under us and pulled us down into it.

I relive this. I have to, because I need to remember her. It was so quick; the water rose around us. Our tent was driving us down stream. I held out my hand for her but she was gone.

I don't know how I survived that. But I was pulled out of that river by a soldier holding out a stick. I remember he placed a blanket about my shoulders and led me to a fire which blazed in a makeshift shelter.

When the dawn came, we realised we had camped in a riverbed. The rain further to the north had caused the dry bed to become full. The rain that fell on us made it worse.

And then it got worse. Much worse. I had no time to think of Idahlia and all those that were lost in the flood because each step I took was an effort. I pleaded then that I die. Many did holler out for their mothers. Many did drop down on that fiery sand and never got up again. I don't know why but I kept going. Everything about that place was hostile. The burning sand, the spiky plants that spat out poison. The burning of our skin. The lack of water, and food.

Then Alexander said we must only march at night. This gave us some respite, and in the day we fought over the scant bush that might shelter us. I was fortunate, for even though I had been swept up in those waters I still wore the cape that I was found in, and I had kept the blanket the kind soldier had given me. I was able to make a kind of bivvy to sleep under.

Then, when was it? Time became nothing. The only thing that mattered was taking one step. Waiting for the dawn and crawling under our rocks. Rocks, blankets, shrubs—it did not matter for all we sought was a shadow and something to wet our lips. Suck on the grass, if you could find some. Lick your sweat, drink your strong urine. Some even scratched themselves to get a drop of blood.

At times Alexander's men would walk by us distributing a few drops of water. They said when it came to him, he would sacrifice his drop to his father, Zeus Ammon. He would look up and ask of that God, his father, the one who did fire a thunderbolt into the womb of his mother, he would say it is you that brings me an heir, now.

But then that God, his father, did his son's bidding, for we came upon an oasis. At first I thought it a mirage. I had had many of those, visions of something inviting me in, a vision showing the other side. The hazy image of something that seemed tangible, but when one drew closer, it disappeared. But this was tangible, and it materialised before us. Real and solid.

There is a spring, date palms. A nomad family shelter us and slaughter most of their flock for us. They advise us with their very brown hands to drink in small mouthfuls, eat in small bites or we might die from taking too much. They are smiles, sunshine, and shelter. They are fresh, delicious water.

The oasis. We rest, sleep and patch up our sunburnt and torn skin. We minister to our feet.

We hear Alexander as he talks of betrayal. How the satraps on the eastern borders of Persia were supposed to bring us fresh supplies. How they must have written us off as dead. And so, on a borrowed camel, Hephaistion and Alexander leave to set the record straight.

On the final night here, we gather what is left of us to walk to the meeting place. Salmous. We are mesmerised by a spectacle. It comes in the form of three maidens walking over a dune. They are dressed only in the orange flowers that surround this oasis. As they come closer I see that the centre figure is Thais, the courtesan. She is flanked by two high-ranking courtesans, Omphale and Xanthe.

The trio make their way to us and there to meet them stands General Ptolemy. He takes Thais' hand and there in that golden light of dusk, the father of the nomad family marries them.

And then we walk again. It is not so easy. And then all goes dark. And I am in the dark brown of the earth.

"Andronicus, when you are well, would you walk to Susa with me?"

I sit in this bed, massaging my toes in preparation for walking, for contemplating what I must do.

"Susa?"

"Yes, my husband is doing much work now to stabilize the land he has conquered. And in Susa he is to unite two peoples. For it is this that gives rise to division. And eventually to anarchy and rebellion."

"I know not of what you speak?"

"Foreigners and then the Greeks. Alexander wishes to unite them permanently through blood."

I have visions now of some slaughter where the bloods of people will be mixed in some kind of pot. I feel my head start to cloud, and my eyes grow tired.

Roxane allows me to doze again. And when I wake she gives me strong wine. It is the wine that is making me strong again, for when I finish the cup I feel as if all my wits have returned.

"You spoke of a mixing of blood?"

"Yes, in Susa, all the royal women and those of noble birth who live either in the great palace there or in the neighbouring satrapies are to be married to the great generals and nobles, the elite soldiers that are grouped here."

I am speechless. I envisage this mass matrimony. I can feel the wretchedness of it. Idahlia's scorn.

"The royal children born of these matches will become half Persian and half Greek. The differences in their opinions and the differences in how they live will be blended and it will reduce the uprisings that are occurring in all the lands Alexander rules over."

I do not mention India, nor Egypt, nor Syria, nor even Asia Minor, which already considers itself a kind of hybrid. What does it matter?

I rake back my hair. It has grown very long, and I have not yet the energy to ask Roxane to cut it for me.

There is something about her that is markedly changed. I cannot think what it is, but it disturbs me.

The man with the fan who squats in the corner of his kindly abode shows me with his two raised fingers that two days have passed. I have been asleep for most of it.

Roxane is present and now she makes me stand and walk. She dresses me in a simple white chiton. She washes my face and combs back my damp hair.

"Why are you doing this?"

"Because it is time for you start living again. Resting now is causing your body to waste away. I have seen this before. If Muni hadn't cajoled my mother, she too would have wasted away. She walked every day, not in fact at the insistence of Muni, but it was as though she was looking for someone, or something. A walk of hope. Hope perhaps kept her alive. But Muni insisted that she mop the floor of our hut each morning and in the evening she made her walk up our incline to fetch pine cones."

"You punish me, Roxane."

"No, I help you, as once you helped me."

"What did we ever do to help you?"

"You spared my life. You pleaded with Alexander to let me live and now my life has turned and opened up again."

"I did no such thing."

"Idahlia told me that it was only because of you and your mercy that Alexander did not hang me."

I find the pain of Idahlia's words, her cruelty, hard. I loved her. And now in my dreams she comes to me as a face. A face whose flesh has been eaten away by fish.

I walk. I am unsteady, but Roxane holds me up. We walk out into the encampment, which is busy with soldiers packing up. Wagons of stores stand waiting to journey on. New uniforms have been brought in and the soldiers once again look like they are ready to battle. The fires, I notice, could do with more dry wood. They smoke too much.

We sit on a bench crafted in fine wood. I run my fingers over the smooth edges of this piece of furniture. I have missed this. The wind ruffles my old hair.

151

"I want to tell you something," she says.

I nod.

"You have work that will pay well. I spoke to Alexander and he needs three hundred gold rings made. In Susa he will place you in a discreet place with a team of fine Persian jewellers and he will supply you with the gold. The treasury there is well stocked."

"Gold rings for what?"

"For the mass marriages that will take place in the grounds of the palace."

"Oh." I rub my hands as if warming them up, making them more supple for this task.

She smiles and takes one of my hands.

"What do you think of this, his wife. Is Alexander taking a wife?" I ask.

"Yes, two. The daughter of King Darius and her cousin. Hephaistion is as well. All the generals are ordered to marry into the royal house of Persia."

"Does it not concern you, that they will produce an heir before you do?"

She looks down at her stomach and pats her womb. "No, no," she says. "My father had two wives. It is common for leaders to have more than one wife, for in doing so, they secure their blood line."

Susa 324 BC

It is monotonous work, tedious. But the ten men I have at my disposable are good at what they do. We are stationed in an artisan workshop set into the walls of the palace. The forge is of good design and there is a place for me to sleep when it gets too dark to work.

The men are cool around me; I can feel their disgust. Gold from the treasury of their former King and ancestors is being used so that Greek men can wed their royal and noble women.

I remain aloof. This will add to the sense that all Greeks are arrogant and have no understanding or tolerance for the thoughts and lives of others. But I don't seem to care. It is as if I have gone beyond needing a family, a group, a sense of belonging. I am Andronicus, me. I crave solitude and the silence that a dark night and the stillness of the earth brings me. I invite nothing in that might disturb this.

I know nothing of the palace outside this gated shop. I see it in the distance, looming white, like a set of gigantic teeth. I believe the gardens are immense and fashioned as if they are still the wild lands. They feature man-made ponds and lakes and staged forests.

One of the men, who speaks some Greek when he chooses to, talks about the large tents being put up on the lawn outside the main building. He scoffs and stares at me, as if I could change this.

We finish the three hundred gold rings with a day to spare. We polish and present them in special boxes made by the tailor in the next house of industry.

I guess I must deliver them and receive my bag of gold, for that is what Roxane promised me on completion. A bag of gold. I don't know if the men who worked with me will receive any form of payment.

The day is abundant with sunshine. The lawns I pass on my way to the entrance of the palace are groomed, and peacocks strut up and down. In the pavilions lights and balloon-like lanterns hang from sturdy ropes above tables laid with white linen. A dais sits at one end, hung with rich curtains of purple. There are three tents, all the same and under this find structures ceremonies of marriage and unification will take place.

The great hall is lined with fine wood and many tapestries. I look up eager to capture the grandeur of such a place and as I stare at its trappings Ptolemy enters through a side door. He sees that I'm carrying a bag and I mouth to him that I have the rings. "All done." I say to him. He opens the canvas bag. "I am to receive payment," I tell the tall General, who is inspecting the rings. His face is impassive; he does not smile, praise or complain.

"Your name?"

"Andronicus, the jeweller, to the royal house of …" I pause, wondering if I should say Macedon, Greece, or Persia. "– the world," I say instead. For I have no desire whatsoever to pander or please.

Ptolemy lets out a laugh. He knows who I am. He knows that my father made small arms for his father Lagus, and if the rumours are true, his real father, Phillip.

"On whose authority do you get paid?"

I don't answer this directly. I pause, making him wait. "Please would you be so kind as to find Roxane for me? The first wife of the King of the World."

He laughs. "The Sogdian girl, she promised you, she would pay you?"

"No, she promised me that her husband, the King, Alexander, would pay me."

Just then Craterus strolls by. His hair is blond, his skin an amber colour, due not to its natural tone but to how much time he spends in the sun's company. He could be Apollo himself, if one was to spread that rumour. He stops and looks over to Ptolemy who holds the rings.

"Ah, the rings, Andronicus. Thank you for doing this. We owe you."

I wait. "A bag of gold I was promised."

"Yes, and a big bag it will be. Just bear with me one moment while I arrange this."

I am about to pack up a small handcart I have found in the back of these quarters. It is well made and sturdy. The handle is wrapped in good thick leather which will make pulling it pleasant. The gold is generous and it lies tucked beneath a false floor I have made at the base of the cart. I am going to Babylon. Why? Because it is a city that hosts many people, and in among the walls of this city and its people one can lose oneself.

I have never really declared myself as a jeweller before, but the word now sits comfortably with me. I have earned the right to claim this title, for I made the royal rings that will, if all goes according to Alexander's plan, proclaim him to be the leader, the ruler, the King of the known world. Well, apart from the place that the Arabians hold, and I am told it is Arabia that Alexander will take next. Then from his new Port in Alexandria, in Egypt, he will establish a navy. So as well as ground troops he will have the sea, and this sea will take him east and west.

There is a small tap at the door, and I am surprised by the person who enters without me even opening it. It is Omphale, a most respected and skilled courtesan. Not that

I would know she's skilled. It is just that I have heard such things.

She is dressed finely in an ensemble that must have come out of the chests of these local princesses. She wears jewels in her hair and her silver bracelet is made of large links.

I stare at it, and she takes it off. "It is beautiful—well, perhaps that is not the right word," she says. "Chain, but solid chain. And it has a special clasp. See here, Andronicus."

I examine the clasp. It sports a snake's head on one side and this head with its forked tongue clips into the tail of another snake. The fitting is spectacular but the execution of the piece is brutish and coarse.

"I have come." She looks back over her shoulder to a young Persian boy who is dragging a large sack behind him. "Come, Saam." The boy deposits the large sack in front of my feet. "My mistress Thais would like you to make a dress for her. She will wear it tomorrow as she observes the weddings."

I start to protest. Omphale opens the sack to reveal pearls, many of them. They spill onto the floor. "She would like it to be made only of pearls, nothing more. It's a simple task of threading them up. That is all; she will wrap this full-sized necklace around her body."

I feel endless fatigue engulf me. My hands ache at the prospect of such a tedious job. I am about to refuse when she hands me a silk purse. "Payment," she says.

I begin as soon as she leaves. The payment is astounding, gems of all kinds, rare and precious, and pearls, many pearls. It is a long day and a long night. I have called back three of the helpers to aid me in this task. They say nothing about the pearls, but it is quite clear they are irritated. I say that this giant necklace is for the wife of General Ptolemy. A friend and … I leave off the fact or fictional part, that he might be the King's older half-brother. It will be of no concern to them, and as I am due to depart this life of following a King around, it is of no concern to me either.

We finish early the next morning. I wrap it in a piece of felt that I find in a chest in the storage cabinet. I lift two or three tools from the drawer in which the felt was kept and place these in my cart. I lift a small hammer from the line-up of hammers and anvils on the work bench. I take some good cotton cloths, a bin of shavings and a bin of bigger filings.

When my cart is packed and I am ready, I make haste to the palace. I want no delays. I want to be on my way to Babylon by noon, and to find a hospitable place to rest on the road. I no longer trust the open road—it is full of bandits, I am told. I need a room.

As I enter the hall I see Roxane. She rushes to me and kisses me on both cheeks. She looks healthy. She wears simple clothes; one might have mistaken her for a gardener. When I mention this, she says it is in the gardens that she spends most of her time now. They are very beautiful, she tells me.

I say that I have a garment for Thais.

"Oh, and you have a cart?"

"Yes, I am going to journey on, Roxane. I am going to find a new place for me to live."

She places her hand to her mouth. I can see that she is upset. I touch her upper arm. I feel something now. Some kind of duty, obligation. But I must not.

"Oh, of course, Andronicus, you must. Many like you are heading back to Greece. General Craterus is to escort the old veterans back to their homeland. It's a good thing."

Just then Omphale appears. She has walked down the grand staircase into the main hall. She takes my upper arm. "Can I see?" she says. I open the corner of the felt. The package is quite hefty.

"I am not sure it will be very comfortable to wear."

"My mistress is one who, when she sets her mind on something, will not be deterred." Omphale takes it from my hands and hurries up the staircase.

Roxane touches my hand, pats my back. "I hope you will be very happy, Andronicus. You have taught me much and for that I am very grateful. I wish you well, I truly do."

Babylon 324 BC

On the road to Babylon I set myself a new set of rules to live by. Not Alexander's, not my father's, but my own, for I crave now a simple life—an elegant life, but a simple life. One where I can dedicate myself to the creation of beautiful small things. I do not wish for a grand home but I do wish for a home.

It's a home I need most; a suitable home where I can work long days and fulfil this new way of being. I will be Andronicus the Jeweller. I will make a home in Babylon where I will make beautiful small objects, jewellery, until the day I die.

I have been in Babylon for only one night, and it is as if the Goddess Athena has journeyed with me, for I find lodgings almost right away. I make a few enquiries with a man whose face looks friendly, who walks near me on a cobbled street. I knock at the suggested door, view the rooms on the ground floor, and they are perfect.

Benjamin is my apprentice, his mother my landlady. The workshop in which we hammer and polish and work with precious metals and fine gems is the place where Benjamin's father worked some time ago, as a stone mason.

The street outside our front window is what I call a parade of the unimaginable. For Babylon is a city of the bizarre. Colourful women with feathers tucked into silk turbans walk tigers on long leads. A man displays a gilt cage in which calls a multi-coloured bird. The snake

charmer on the corner calls all to see how he can make
his snake dance with one tune from his reed pipe.

We never cook; instead we buy food from the
vendors one lane over. We eat out in the cobbled streets
at well-set tables, and drink whatever is the latest brew to
be discovered. My landlady, Beulah, is partial to a flask
of distilled herbs gathered, she says, from the fields in
Phoenicia. She tells me that the drink has properties that
bring one's fantasies to life.

We work well, Benjamin and I, and our best sellers are
the collars we make for the exotic pets that the
Babylonians are so fond of.

With the jewels from the bag from Thais, we
make fine-studded collars with real gems. Our business
grows and soon we are taking orders. Benjamin draws
well and is able to divine what our clients most want,
drawing out in front of them as they describe what is on
their minds. We take a deposit, now, to buy the materials
and we pride ourselves that our people always walk out of
the shop satisfied with our work and their new
investment.

This morning Benjamin arrives early. He resides above
the workshop with his mother. He is earnest when I see
him, his head bowed, engaged in the piece he has in hand.

I see that the chain he is making is not dissimilar
to the bracelet chain that Omphale wore, but the links he
is making are of fine gold. He grins and shows me his
drawing.

It is of a bracelet, and from the links hang small
objects.

"Show me the clasp?" I say.

He does not hesitate to point out a bolt. A small piece of rod that inserts into a larger ring.

"See this," he says. "It's a tooth from my sister. When it came out of her mouth she was very sad. So I told her that one day I would make something from it."

He points to one of the small drawn objects. It is gilt cage, and inside it is a small bird. "A dove," he says.

"I have not met your sister."

"No, Chana lives in the place beyond the river."

I don't say anything else; I don't want to pry. But he goes on as if he needs to tell me about her, about them.

"She lives with my father. He left, you know. He said he was called by our people to rebuild the temple. So he left his workshop here where he made fine things out of stone, and fine items for my mother's business, and he took Chana."

"Was your mother sad about this?"

"Yes, a little, but for Chana it is a better life for her over there. For Chana does not hear. And my mother felt that my father should take her each day to the site. There she could help the builders with their work. She loves being outside, she loves birds."

Benjamin continues to work. Then he looks up. "Andronicus, she could not be trained in the art of midwifery for she faints at the sight of blood, and when my mother tried to teach her how to sew well she was always cutting herself with the shears and pricking herself with the needle."

He squints and lowers the small circles of chain to our large lamp. He pinches its sides together and now he will heat the join to make it secure. "She is not like us, Andronicus, she is a little different. That is why she needs a different life. My mother says she likes the way the tools touch the stone' when the hammer is noisy, she can feel it in her bones, in her heart and it makes her happy."

Opis 324 BC

A storm brews in Opis, and Alexander has stated that the
generals and their entourage are to be housed in the old
palace there. But many insects, rodents and dead leaves
have made their home here among the dust and decay.

"Totally unsuitable," Ptolemy says.

Alexander shuts the general down with his hand
and a shake of the head. "We'll make this our temporary
headquarters while the rest camp outside the gates. The
veterans will take the best site, for it is them that we are
farewelling tomorrow, and they must have the best food,
the best wine, and the best place to pitch their tents."

The wind is loud and it roars within the cavernous
hall. All is gone; there are no furnishings. Looters have
smashed glass and fittings, birds nest in the beams, moss
grows up the front steps and climbing plants have crawled
their way in.

When the eunuch shows her to the room set aside
for her and her husband, she feels faint. She holds her
stomach. She retches as though the child is still within
her. The eunuch comes to her and crouches. "It's foul.
Why does he insist we stay here?"

She looks up into his baggy face; dark circles rim
his eyes. Like all of them, life has become a matter of
making do, of trying to contain oneself and of being
reasonable, for the King's temper flares often.

"Does it hurt?" He points to her empty womb. "I
mean."

The eunuch is one of the very few that know that
the baby came out all blood and not made, for her
husband appointed him to watch over her while she made

a home in the head gardener's house in the grounds of Susa. How she had liked it there. She felt she knew the man that lived there, even though he had vacated the place for her.

His tools were mounted on the wall, hooks holding them secure. They were clean and polished. The ones he used most, like his spade, his fork and his cutting implements were placed in an exact line on the white wall of his living area, as a middle row. Those he used less often were placed in a high row above, and those of medium use were lined up horizontally on the bottom row. His boots were polished, six of them, and sat on three shelves of marble by the front door. His coats hung on a wooden rack.

His fire blazed and she drank warm wine and enjoyed the eunuch's company.

The room in Opis reeks of death. They find the source; the stench causing them both to gag. Roxane holds a cloth to her nose and mouth and picks up the dead, black-feathered bird with her fingers.

The eunuch does not follow her as she moves with its dripping carcass down the large staircase and into the kitchen below. She opens the door and throws the rotting corpse out to the long grass.

As she returns, she sees her husband in fervent talks with Perdicass. She does not care for this general much, and it is obvious that most of them care little for her. She stands and listens.

"I have given you all I can give, Alexander," the oversized, crusty general says.

"You must have gold hoarded in that palatial house of yours, Perdicass. Gold that Craterus can access and give to these men who have served us well."

"Served us well? All they have done is complain and garner contempt for you. They have revolted and rebelled and now they are ridden with disease and broken bodies they come begging for compensation."

"I want to reward them for their service."

She sees Perdicass wring his hands, hears him crack his knuckles. "I assure you, Alexander, I hoard no gold or anything precious, and I will honour my promise to divide up my land so that these, veterans can retire in comfort."

Alexander thanks the general, muttering as he exits the room in which Perdicass is now seated, helping himself to a large mug of poor wine.

Even the wine is unpleasant now. The stocks arriving are few and far between and the cup bearers have had to make it last by adding much water and some of the local drinks.

That night she sits on the floor of this large room. It would have been fancy in its day. The copper bath would have been polished to a high sheen. Servants would have filled it with hot water and the royal occupants would have soaked in fine herbs and oils.

The eunuch has swept a path of tiled floor for her to sleep on. Alexander will not be coming. He doesn't come at nights.

It is Craterus' last night. She can't help herself. She sneaks out of the palace and down the small rise to where the veterans' camp is situated.

She thinks back on the day as she creeps further and further into the camp she once knew. The one where she was another person entirely. She thinks of the rowdy last meeting that Alexander endured with these departing soldiers. Back when she was travelling overland at Craterus' side, she found these men to be good. Loyal. Wise. But today she witnessed something different. They had heckled her husband, thrown rocks at him. And finally he had had Ptolemy find the ring leaders. Right there and then he had guards behead them. It was an awful sight. Her husband had stomped off.

And here they sleep. Their wish to return home has been granted, but their protest was about not being honoured or appreciated. Their long service goes unrewarded. Alexander must have felt some guilt about this, for she did hear him earlier on talking with Perdicass who, according to the eunuch, is the only general left who has a family fortune waiting for him. So he is making all this possible.

She waits outside Craterus' tent. She can see Nico wiping plates down, storing them between good linen and placing them in leather bags. She is about to turn back when Nico sees her.

He moves to Craterus' side and taps him on the shoulder and then he points to her.

"It's you," Craterus says.

"Yes."

"You shouldn't be here."

"No. But I am. I just came to say goodbye."

"Nico …"

"Yes, sir, of course. I will patrol, we don't want intruders and their eyes setting foot anywhere near."

Craterus encloses her in an embrace. They stand silent like that. She rests her head on his shoulder, inhales his leathery scent. "Is a dead black bird a bad omen?" Somehow omens seem to consume the lives of the Greeks.

"Why do you ask?"

She tells him about the bird. The eunuch said was a raven.

"Well, it was ravens that lined the path to the oracle that we visited in Siwah. They were our guides, and their presence told us in which direction to put our feet, for a sand storm had made us blind."

"So that is good, then, isn't it? For that is where he learnt of his divine birth. Where the seer told him that he would be the first of three great Kings of the world."

"Yes. But there is another story about ravens that might interest you." He sits down and pulls her onto his lap. "Once the raven was white. And one day Apollo sent a raven out to spy on his lover, Coronis. The raven duly returned and told Apollo that Coronis was lying with another. Apollo flew into a rage and he hunted Coronis down and shot her with his bow and arrow. He also cursed the raven. He turned their feathers black."

She feels her body grow rigid. He kisses her neck. Craterus stands and walks to the open door. "If you were free I would take you back with me. But Roxane, you are not free, neither of us are free."

She feels a lump in her throat.

"Would you take me, if I was not married to the King?"

"If you were not married to the King, I would take you, even if you were married to someone else, I would hide you away here in my belongings and take you. I have a wife at home, but I would forsake her for you."

"How does Alexander differ from any other man?"

"Roxane –" he pauses. "I took an oath as a soldier of the Greek army. And when I recited those words, they were words of honour and trust. I spoke of never bringing shame upon the King."

She lets her tears fall. He speaks so well; so honestly.

"Can you tell me the oath so that I may take it too?"

He places her hand upon her heart. "Say these words after me." He wipes away her tears with his fingers.

"I promise to obey and stand by the King. To fight for the King and uphold the laws that the King does make. I swear to honour all those among us who are loyal to the King and I promise to the death to fight for the rights of my people. To never desert them or bring our nation into disrepute. I am a man of honour, a servant of the King, a protector of the nations and of all those who come under his command."

She repeats the words; his hands hold hers.

"Today, your men were not loyal to Alexander, they cursed him."

Craterus shakes his head. "They were not my men."

She takes his arm, turns so that her back rests on his lean torso. "How so?"

"They were plants, Roxane, men placed in the rows of my old veterans."

He holds her fast and then releases her and turns her towards him. He starts to whisper. "Roxane, there is much danger. Traitors, and those who have stolen much from Alexander. Men of trust I believe have taken what is not theirs to take. Watch out for it. For among those that appear most loyal can be a wolf in the clothing of a sheep. Alexander refuses to see it, even though I have warned him of it."

"Why is it you then that has to go? Why does he not keep you close to protect him?"

"Because he trusts me with the most valuable asset we have, that of the homeland. That of the united states of Greece. The centre of our world and the world which will grow under his command. He may want to rule from Egypt, which has many strategic advantages, but it is Macedonia where still much of the power lies.

We must have the support of our own peoples or we have nothing."

"So what is it you will do there?"

"I will relieve the tired and elderly Antipater, who is holding it tight for the King. But he has started to complain of the King's neglect, of his abandonment."

"I understand," she says.

"Not many see a homeland as love. They see a person, a pet perhaps, a lover, but not many recognise that in the lands of one's people is planted their love. And it is this that I must go back to and make sure we never lose our connection with our roots. It is there that I must find the resourcing to fund whatever mad idea your husband has next."

"Why fund a mad man?"

"Because, Roxane, Little Star, your husband is a genius. If you had seen his mind working out the ways in which to conquer an enemy much more powerful than us, then you would know this is the work of someone who is not born like many of us; this is someone born with a special kind of intelligence. A special gift that we must appreciate, for without a man like Alexander we would not have discovered many things."

"He flew to the top of our rock."

Craterus smiles. "Yes, he did."

Roxane begins to leave but then she turns. "Our child. I laid it to rest in a nest high in a tree in the forest of Susa. When the flood came out of me, I saw in its waters a thing that reminded me of the shell imprint and the little fish that found its way into the rock. I left the rock in the nest beside it."

"I know," Craterus says. He pokes his head out of the tent and in a whisper calls back Nico. "Escort her back and pay the eyes."

Ectabana 324 BC

They were supposed to be striking out to Babylon. There had been much concern that Alexander needed to become more responsible. There was talk of rebellion within the satrapies, the Indians not paying their taxes and the people at home baying for his blood. Roxane heard the rumours.

"I have warned him, my love, warned him, why we walk now to Ectabana and not the heart of Persia I do not know," the eunuch says.

"He says he needs to rest. That the fresh air and not the stuffy air of Babylon will be good for him."

The eunuch huffs. "And he has picked all the pretty boys and those with Herculean bodies to accompany us. Games. Games. Do you know about the Greek Games?"

Roxane does not.

"Well wait and see. They are to my mind a great indulgence. Meeting strength against strength, vanity against vanity." The eunuch points to her husband who is riding up ahead on a new white horse, about to enter the palace gates of Ectabana. The palace was built for the Persian kings long ago so they could find some relief from the summer heat.

It soon becomes apparent that this palace is a place of beauty. It is well maintained and appears to have one large family overseeing the running, maintenance and service. The family are of small build with large smiles and much willing.

The eunuch assigns her an apartment on the side furthest away from the oval field on which the men play.

It does not worry her; in fact she is relieved to have some time to bathe and cleanse herself, to make sure her hair is well cared for and her feet and hands are rubbed free of the callouses that have gathered there.

They have been there two nights when she is woken from a deep sleep. She hears something, feels something. The curtain that surrounds her bed is billowing in and out. But the doors are shut and there is no wind. She smells spring flowers, feels an unearthly chill.

You must rise at dawn. She knows this voice. It has spoken to her before. *Yes Roxane, it is me, I am dead...... I cannot touch you and clean out your womb, which insists on being cloggy...... But I can tell you what you must do...... You must go down to the kitchens below. There on a shelf up high you will find a pot of rose petal jam...... Take it.*

The voice fades a little but then finds its strength again. *Go to the stables and take a horse...... Ride out of the palace grounds...... Ride east until you see four trees in a row...... Turn to the south...... Ride until you see a small hut...... Three women wait for you...... They will point to the statues...... You will rub the jam on the noses of these lions.*

The curtains still. The room is not so cold now. She speaks to the voice, but it is gone. She knows the voice well. It is the voice of the Rajah's wife.

As if driven by another force, something beyond her control, she rises at dawn and does as the voice told her to do. It is not hard; everything happens without fuss or bother. Even the groom hands her a horse as if he had known she would come. She rides out beyond the palace gates. The wind is warm in her hair, the horse swift and obedient. She finds the four trees, and then changes to the south where she finds the women who all sit in a row on old chairs outside a hut that needs repair. One of the women stands and comes to her. She holds the reins of the horse as she dismounts and leads them both to a pair of stone lions. The woman, who wears an old blue scarf and whose clothes are black, nods to her. Roxane applies the rose-petal jam to the noses of the two stone animals. Lions.

When Roxane returns, the gardens are draped in the shadows of the night. She is no sooner out of the stable when someone snatches her arm.

"Where were you?" It is Thais.

"I have been out riding."

"All day?"

"Yes." Roxane feels as if she has done something wrong. Ptolemy walks towards them. He is angry. She can tell that something has happened.

"I have asked her; she says she was out of the palace all day," Thais says.

Ptolemy arches an eyebrow and says she must follow him.

"What has happened?"

"You don't know what has happened?" Ptolemy's tone is harsh. What has she done, unknowingly, to create such hostility?

"No, I—"

"He's dead."

"Who is dead?" Roxane immediately thinks of her husband. His poor spirits, his irrational behaviour, his irritability at everyone and everything. What happened? Was he killed? Did he drop dead due to the wounds that seem to open up from time to time? Wounds from the many battles he has survived.

"Hephaestion," Thais snaps.

She is relieved that it is not Alexander, for as much as he is unpredictable and rash, of late he has been good to her.

"Did you kill him? It would suit you well to have had him killed," Thais says.

Ptolemy holds his wife back, to prevent her from coming any closer to Roxane.

"No, I did not."

"Then prove to us that you did not."

Roxane thinks hard, her heart is racing. She says to them, "Come."

She leads them to the stable where the groom that attended to her is sitting on a stool. He is drinking a hot steaming cup of soup and stands as they enter. He bows to Ptolemy.

"She says she has been riding all day?" Ptolemy says, pointing at Roxane.

"Yes, she has. She rode out at dawn and has just returned."

"What was so necessary for her to be out all day? Did she meet someone; did she pay someone who plotted to kill our Hephaestion?"

The groom shakes his head. He takes Ptolemy to the horse. "The horse has worked hard, his coat is still moist. The Lady Roxane, our Queen, she rode him far. It was a journey of some importance, I believe, for she met the ladies of the lions."

Thais claps her hands. "Enough."

The groom calls up a small boy. "Bibi, tell the good general what you saw."

The boy is slow to speak, nervous. "The Queen, she did ride out east, then she took a turn south at the four trees. She rode south to the stone lions."

Thais is impatient. "This is convenient. A good alibi."

The boy talks. "My brother asked me to follow her, to keep her safe. There are many bandits about, robbers, and we needed to make sure she would return without harm. But of course she would be protected, for the good spirits fly today. And it is this that kept her safe."

"Upon the head of Dionysus, please speak plainly."

The groom interjects. "This custom, well it is good for women who desire to be with child."

Ptolemy huffs. Sighs. "So she interacted with no one except some stone lions."

"Yes, and the ladies of the lions. No one else," the boy, Biba, says.

Roxane barges through the barriers that have been put in place inside the palace. She comes to a guarded corridor and the guards prevent her from going any further.

"Let me see him. Let me see my husband."

They push her back.

"Let me in." She is tired and hot, and her hands are still sticky from the jam. She slumps down the wall and places her head in her hands. Hephaestion was neither nice, nor horrible to her. He was just there. Always there, beside Alexander.

A voice comes from a door further along. "Let her in."

She enters this small room. Her husband lies in a tangle of sheets. The room smells of wine and stale sweat. His eyes are red and inflamed.

"I'm so sorry that this has happened."

Alexander drags her down so that she sits beside him on the narrow bed.

"What happened?"

"He was not well. I ordered the doctor to ensure he did not drink any wine for three days, nor did he eat. I asked that he take only the bitter herbs and drink water."

"Did someone kill him?"

Alexander turns to her, his eyes wide. "Yes, in a way."

"Ptolemy and Thais think I might have killed him. How could I have killed him? Did I do anything to harm him?"

Alexander inhales. "No, no, not you. That boy and the doctor, they should have watched him."

Alexander lies back down and cries. He turns to her. "It was their fault. They should have stopped him. But they were not by his side when he ordered a guard to bring him chicken, not one but two whole chickens and a flask of strong wine."

She waits for him to recover his breath. He takes her hands and squeezes them till she can feel her bones crunching. "Roxane, he ate and he drank. And then he collapsed and died."

"It was not poison?"

"No, it was the chicken and the wine. He always took too much wine. The humours were all amuck. I was trying to get them back in balance for him. But … sometimes he did not want to listen to me."

She listens to her husband talk of his lover, of the one he loved the most. "He was always by my side. He did not want me only because I was the King, or a conqueror. He was not one of those sycophants, always trying to please me. Weak and despairing and sickly. He was the one who told me what I needed to hear."

Alexander lies his head down on the bed. "I need to rest now," he says.

She glides past the guards who look her up and down.

When she returns to her room, her bed is not turned down nor her bath run. So the whole palace mourns Hephaestion. She thinks how this family are the palace, how they have made it so that every inch of it shines: the silver and turquoise tiles that cover the roof of this dark wooden place; the door handles of brass, the silver urns. Everything like a mirror that one can see oneself in. The gardens of soft beauty, flowing vines and green shrubs shaped so that they look like rocks, or towers.

But when she lies down upon the creased covers, one of the girls who attend her comes in. She fluffs about. Her demeanour is not happy; she is angry, flippant in her gestures and talk.

"What is it?" Roxane says. "You mourn Hephaestion?"

"No, I mourn my brother. He strung him up."

"Who strung him up?"

"Alexander. He hung him and the Greek doctor in the small place where we collect the flowers. Where our flowers dry, their blood drips. My father has not the courage to cut him down. My mother is tearing out her hair in grief."

Roxane heart sinks. She takes the girl whose name she does not know by the hand. "I'm sorry. It was your brother that was appointed to help the doctor care for Hephaestion?"

"Yes, he was so proud to have been asked. So honoured."

"Go now to your parents, be with them."

Roxane finds the eunuch. "Come," she says to him, and walks out with the small man dressed now in black silk. His turban sports a black feather. She wonders if it is the feather of a raven.

"Where are we going?"

"It's not pleasant, but we need to do this."

She finds the little place, almost a replica of the main one, except its exterior is built of white wood and its roof is made of copper and red tiles. She enters to find the bodies of both the doctor and the boy hanging.

"Help me cut them down."

"I don't think we should be doing this."

"If you don't help me, I will do it on my own."

She climbs a ladder and with a swift movement releases the dead weights from their knots. They are light souls, not men of mass, and she is able to cradle each one.

Roxane places them on the floor inside this scented bower. It is a fitting place, unlike the mourning tent. The eunuch brings her some water, and she wipes the signs of death from the bodies. Gently Roxane wraps them in linen cloths that have been used to dry lavender.

"Now have some guards come and take the boy to his family, and the doctor to the woods. Lay him out under the trees."

Exhausted, yet unable to sleep, Roxane sips warm boiled water. The taste of it is welcome, as if it is rinsing out all that is within. She closes her eyes. The voice is with her again, bringing with it the winter snow of her youth.

Go, now, deep down into the bowels of this place...... Walk to the end of the damp dark corridor...... Go towards the light...... A spirit flies tonight.

She is gone again. The frost lifts. And in the Rajah's wife's wake is the scent of spring flowers. She inhales their fragrance and wipes the air with her hand as if trying to clear the curtain between what is up in the sky and what is down here on earth.

Her feet start to move. They obey the words. She runs downstairs, turning a corner, a small landing, more stairs, until there are no more steps in front of her. She finds the space here musty, old, and dark. Sconces provide her with some light and she walks to the end where she can see lots of bright light.

She comes upon a circular room, and inside are twelve large candles.

In the centre there is a stone plinth, and on it lies her husband, beside him the dead Hephaestion. Her husband holds the marble-like face of his lover, his tears washing the body of the deceased.

She places herself beside her husband. He clasps her close to him.

The Road to Babylon 324 BC

They move now to Babylon. Alexander has ordered that Hephaestion's body be placed in a barrel of honey. He has centred this barrel on the leading wagon.

They have barely started their journey when a swarm of wasps congregates around the barrel. Alexander stops the train. He mounts the wagon and begins to slap the wasps with his hands. No one does anything to stop this madness.

Roxane orders a guard to drag him away from the stinging pests. She asks that water be boiled and that they pour water over the barrel. When every wasp is dead, she nods to Ptolemy.

They begin their march again.

On the third day, they are attacked by bandits, who demand they hand over anything of value. Alexander walks up to the leader; he is very close to him. "Do you not know who I am?"

"A Greek, an invader. A thief."

Roxane sees her husband's anger flare. It is as if everything around him turns red. She rushes to try to intervene, but she is too late. He has slashed the man's throat with a small knife. He has gouged out the eye of another. The guards now attack, and they do not spare one life.

But Alexander does not leave them there on that road. He has not finished with them. He walks up to every dead body and stamps on their heads. The sound of him smashing their skulls is terrible.

Two days later they approach Babylon. A number of the Magi come out and greet them, and beg Alexander to refrain from entering the city at this time. The omens are unfavourable.

Alexander sits, and as the Magi return through the beautiful Ishtar gates, he closes his eyes and balls his hands.

He calls his seer. "Aristander."

Ptolemy comes forward.

"I called for my seer, not you, Ptolemy."

"I know this, Alexander, but I have information."

"Pray tell."

"You donated some funds to the Magi, did you not?"

"Yes, very generous we were."

"To restore the ziggurat and the hanging gardens to their former glory."

"Yes. Indeed. Babylon is a fine city, and it will be an even finer city by the time I have finished with it."

"Well, it seems the Magi have squandered your funds and none of the work has been carried out."

Alexander walks around his camp. He checks every tent and every patch of land as if looking for some answer. "Roxane," he finally yells.

They wander off. "What do you think?" he asks her.

"We have not seen this for ourselves. The Magi are holy people bound by certain sacred oaths and laws. Should you not talk to them directly about this before they are condemned?"

"Call back the Magi," he shouts to the throng who are standing around.

The Magi arrive just before dark. They look like a flock of white butterflies in their long white robes, and they bring good food and good wine. Many are elderly. They sit while Alexander questions them.

"Has the work been carried out on the ziggurat and the gardens? These are the instructions I left with you, along with the funding to make this happen."

"It's been difficult, King Alexander, but we have started with the repairs."

"Why has it been difficult?"

"Many of our good stone masons come from the place across the river, and they have been called upon to work on a temple there. But we have managed to find a company of men from Egypt, and they have proved to be valuable in their labours."

"So the work will be carried out."

"Yes, it will," the head Magi says. He is very elderly, and he looks up as the stars start to appear in the sky. "We warn you because we care for you. Babylonians are very loyal to the crown of Macedonia. We see up there some odd times, times of uncertainty, of change, of carnage. So that is why we advise you to not advance yet into our city. Maybe take a trip to Pella, to your country of birth, to steady the waters there."

The campsite retires. Everyone tries to sleep as best they can. The grass is long on this stretch of flat land and it scratches the skin. The insects crawl in its tall shelter. Alexander falls asleep beside his wife. Roxane hardly sleeps; she listens to the uneven breathing of her husband.

The day dawns and it seems as if everyone is packed and ready to move. Many believe he, Alexander, will take the Magi's advice but on rising Alexander stands on a wagon deck.

"Aristander," Alexander says. "Read the omens." Alexander jumps down from the wagon, landing awkwardly on his feet. He has hurt his left ankle but he continues to walk on regardless, as though he has no pain at all.

The seer finds a clear patch of grass and takes an old dog, one of the many that follow them. He waits for his knife to be sharpened before slitting the dog's throat. The sticky blood flows out onto the little patch of green grass. He lies the dog down parallel to the north wall of the city, then kneels down and slits the dog's belly open and with the tip of his knife pulls out the entrails.

He sits with the omen for some time before he addresses Alexander. "My King, the left lobe is diseased. It would be unwise to enter the city." Aristander points to the Ishtar gate.

Alexander rubs his chin, the dimple there now roughened with whiskers, unshaven and coarse. His blue eyes are less bright.

"Is there a back gate?" he asks. "What does the right lobe of this liver say?"

"My King." Aristander kneels again, as the flies begin their buzz around an unexpected meal. "It is clear, King Alexander." His eyes travel to the right end of the north wall.

A guard nearby shouts out that there is a back gate.

"Well, we shall enter the city presently. Through the back gate, my friends."

The Babylonian Court 323 BC

Benjamin sweeps up the dust and filings of the day. He shuts the market window and begins to turn their sign around when a small man knocks at the closed door.

He knocks a second time, and Benjamin opens it. I hear the knock, dreading that it is yet another customer wanting something made in too quick a time. We have some ready-made stock, but it is always the custom-made pieces that are in demand.

I sigh, a sigh which only I hear, and make my way through to the workshop. Benjamin introduces the visitor as a man from the court. He is the Persian eunuch, still dressed in fine clothes. Today I admire his single gold earring and a turban of peach-coloured silk.

"I'm here to ask that you may be of service to us."

I nod. My wine calls me, and I am keen to fill my stomach with some meat and flat bread.

"The King has asked that you might make some clothes for his wife."

"Which wife?" I remember that he now has three wives.

"Oh, the beauty Roxane, who else?"

"Did he not bring the Persian princesses with him?"

"Oh no, they are in Susa. Left there, where they belong."

"No heir yet, then?"

"No, I don't believe so."

"Well I'm no longer in the business of clothing royals, but I can make up some jewellery for Roxane." As I finish speaking, Beulah walks in.

"This man has come asking for clothes for the Queen," Benjamin says.

Beulah blinks, and turns to get a better look at this agent of the crown.

"I think we can manage that? Can we not, Andronicus?"

The eunuch tips his head and touches his turban, as if this seals some kind of deal. He takes from his pocket a felt bag and deposits it on our counter.

"Tomorrow, mid-morning. I will greet you at court. Side door."

Beulah carries a covered basket, and I carry a great deal of resentment. I don't want anything to do with this. I am an independent jeweller with my own clientele. We wait in the tiled room below. The walls are peach coloured, and there are many palms in terracotta pots. The place echoes when one speaks. Although it's grand, it's in need of redecorating.

The sound of feet—feet above, feet below, feet on the balconies—gives us hope, that soon we will be in talks about the new garments. But no, we wait.

Eventually the bright little eunuch comes, apologising for keeping us waiting. Mid-morning for some who rise early has been and gone. For those of us who like our beds, it is now. But it appears she has gone already.

"A servant who attends to her chamber says she waited down here earlier on with great hopes of seeing you, Andronicus," says the eunuch. He sighs, as if he carries a great weight on his shoulders. "But like many things around here at the moment, one thing is said, another is done; one thing is done and the act of it denied.

———

One hires a scribe to write a list only to find that the scribe is summoned back to rewrite the list."

"We will postpone the meeting until another day," Beulah says. "For you see I have many other costumes to cut and stitch and deliver, and my time is precious."

"No, no—please, I have sent many servants out to search for her. She is something of a stray, as we might say. She takes herself off with neither word nor consideration. But I do know where she likes to go, so I expect her to greet you any moment now."

The eunuch is not wrong, for just then Roxane appears. She still wears the dress of the gardener. Her hair long and unkempt, and she carries a monkey on her hip.

"Sorry about this. Sorry, my mistake." She rushes to me and kisses my cheek. "I just took this little fellow to the gardens so he could play in a real tree." She wanders over to the nearest potted palm and fingers the leaves. I see her take a caterpillar from a large, spiked leaf. She squashes it between her fingers and feeds the animal. "They pull out their teeth; it is so cruel, to take from any animal the very thing that it needs to exist in the wild. The tigers, you know, the ones they parade up and down, they remove all their teeth and their claws as well. The lions too."

"Right, now, there we have it. New clothes for the woman who will sit beside our King." The eunuch pulls up a chair. He sits and orders Roxane to stand still and be measured. He claps his hand and a boy in a room brings over a screen.

When Beulah opens her basket I see the familiar coiled ribbons and a pair of shears. She disappears with Roxane behind the screen while we wait and try to chat.

"You know that Alexander is to bring the great man Antipater to Babylon?"

I didn't know, but the poor chap deserves a break from the mammoth effort of keeping the states of Greece content. Even when I lived there, feuds would erupt—all kinds of disputes and rivalries.

"Yes, he brings him here to bestow the honour of Satrap on him. A reward for his loyalty and tireless efforts. Holding the fort at home. Not for the faint hearted. But I imagine he will enjoy the splendour of Babylon. Yes indeed."

"And who will govern the home states once Antipater is relieved of his duty?"

"Oh, Craterus will. You know the King refers to him as the strongest. A good man, is Craterus."

I nod, and try to distract myself by counting the palms. Twenty-five in all, dotted around this cavernous room.

"You know Perdicass thought that he should get the title of Governor of the home states, or Vizier as he likes to call it. He was certain it would go to him. After all, it is his fortune that the King has used lately to finance the ongoing costs of running countries. It is quite some cost. And with all the looting of the treasuries, and the dishonest men who have defrauded him and embezzled the taxes collected and other revenues from trade and the like—well, it's horrendous."

"Sometimes biggest is not best," I say.

"Well, Andronicus, I must agree with you there. Yes, a simple life is a rich life. That is what my mother always said."

They appear, having hardly spoken behind that screen. I tried to listen; it was better than listening to the man in front of me. But Beulah works in silence. She has pinned the ribbons to the drawing of Roxane.

"So, what will you make for her?" the eunuch asks.

"What she needs the most. I am sure Beulah has taken note of Roxane's needs."

"We need to make the waist of any costume so that it can be let out. We need to make sure she has enough room to grow," says Beulah.

The eunuch says nothing. I look up to the highest balcony. Roxane looks baffled.

"My dear, you are with child."

"How do you know?"

"I come from a line of midwives. My mother, her mother. And so I know when someone is carrying. When did you last bleed?"

Roxane shrugs. "But this is normal for me, not to bleed, since my life has become one of travelling and uncertainty."

"As it does, for you carry no extra fat on you, and the inconsistency that is weaved into a life of hardship and survival means that the blood cycle is disrupted. Yet you can still conceive. And you have."

"When is she due?" the eunuch says.

"Mid-year. In the heat of summer, the humid days."

"And is it a boy?"

Beulah closes her eyes. "My grandmother had the gift for divining the gender of a child in the womb. Give me a strand of your hair, my dear, and I will see if I can remember how she did this."

Roxane pulls out a long strand of her hair. She asks Roxane for the ring that she wears on her forefinger. It is one of the plain gold bands I made for the wedding ceremonies in Susa.

"Lie here on this couch and raise your top."

Roxane does as Beulah says and soon Beulah is making the ring on the strand of hair spin above the tiny rise that is her stomach. The spinning gets faster. Then Beulah stops its orbit.

"You see, it spins from east to west. Not north to south. The circle around the Earth, not over the Earth. We need both circles to live, to be. But the one that stays warm and dry in the circular sphere, where the food grows best and the seas meet, well that is the masculine one."

"What energy is it if it spins the other way, up and down, so to speak," the eunuch says.

Beulah smiles. "The female can sustain much hardship—labour, for instance. She bears the pain of all her children, no matter how small or grown-up they become. She is the one who keeps her child warm. It is she who is able to sustain life in the coolest of climates. She is the one of fortitude."

Beulah's Room 323 BC

Until now I have never set foot in the room where Beulah sews and lives. It is lofty. A large cutting table is at the centre, and a window giving ample light faces the hub of Babylon. On one side a shelving unit hosts all things needed in the craft of tailoring. On the other side is a marble basin set on black table with refreshments. In an alcove to the rear, a curtain separates Beulah and Benjamin's quarters from her working space.

I see three stone statues, looking like goddesses, standing naked in one corner. Fabric is draped over their bodies.

"Oh, my husband made them for me," she says. "It saves so much fitting time. The three are quite different in body shape, so I can gauge the best fit for my client without remeasuring."

I remain silent, stunned by their incredible beauty, the perfect solution for her. Time saving and accurate, efficient and magnificent.

"He is a very good stone mason, my husband."

"Do you miss him?"

"Every day."

"Then why, why …"

"Am I apart?" She pours us a drink, guides me to one of her armchairs and we sit opposite sipping the strong drink she so likes. "Well, you shouldn't ever prevent a person from doing what they are called to do. I am called to do this. He was called to help in the land of our forebears."

She hands me a stuffed plump fig. Inside is a sweet soft cheese. I eat while she talks. "My father built this business from nothing. He had an obsession with fabric, with the fine bone needles, with thread, and with any kind of bauble he could find to complement an outfit and enhance a person's natural looks, no matter the gender. I would sit here, in this very room and watch him at work; I would copy him with pretend shears, a pretend needle, until, at last, he said I may assist him."

"And your mother was a midwife?"

"Yes, my maternal line, this is what they do. They have served in many courts all over Persia—Egypt, even. They are sought out by nobles and royalty."

I go to speak of Sarah, but something silences me. I feel tired. The weariness of the past is best left there.

"And Andronicus, it was good fortune, or fate, whatever you would like to call it. But when you came along, a jeweller, well that is what Benjamin was drawn to. He was making beaded necklaces when he was just four. Finding odd things in the street, lost items; buying glass beads when he had a few coins in his pocket."

Beulah pours another drink, but I intend not to drink it. I shift it to one side as she talks about the designs. Of what we should make. I start to mumble about blues and whites, shifts. Pale blue for the mother to be.

Beulah shuts me down. "No, no, Andronicus, we must clothe her in armour. Not in the attire of a weepy goddess, but in clothes that make her look formidable."

I try to imagine Roxane in the clothes of a soldier, and I take up some charcoal and begin to draw the uniform I am familiar with. She stills my hand. And shakes her head.

"No, not of a lowly soldier, but of an Amazonian." She heads to the shelves that store her fabric. She takes a bolt of grey silk and drapes it over the second-tallest stone statue. "She must be strong and visible. I can see her already in this silk, with wide silver bangles going right up to her elbow. She needs a trim of white fur. Do you see, Andronicus?"

I take a sip. I need to visualise what she is describing, and little by little, as she starts to fashion the fabric into unsewn garments, I can see her vision.

A coat of silver silk, lined with cream with a hood that drapes far down her back. A long, black coat of wool with gold buttons and deep pockets. Leather trousers. A dark blue dress of silk with pearls that drape down to her navel, many strings of them, and soft snakeskin boots that come up over the knee.

The Balcony Overlooking The River

323 BC

Alexander is not well. Roxane holds his hand as he lies on their vast bed that overlooks the sleepy river. The doors are wide open for he is so hot. One minute hot, the next minute shivering, so she wraps him up in a blanket and asks for the heated stones.

He can no longer visit the baths; he is too weak.

She wears her new clothes, which pleases him, and she holds his hand to her stomach when the child inside moves. It brings tears to his eyes.

He speaks of when Antipater arrives; how marvellous it will be for he will be less burdened by all these affairs of the state. Then he tells her that they will move to Alexandria, in Egypt. He is building a magnificent city; the palace is nothing like anyone has ever seen before. And in this city of trade and industry, of the naval base, there will be not only a library but an academy where their sons will be educated by great minds.

Seven days pass, and they hear that the train of Antipater will soon arrive. Alexander rallies; he is able to sit in the throne room and sign certain laws. He is vocal with his thoughts. He makes plans with Ptolemy, that they will invade Arabia in the autumn months. He is drawing all the time, sketching the harbour in Alexandria, which includes a tower in which a fire will burn eternally, guiding the boats into this safe harbour. He draws up new military bases that will be established as far west as Massilia. He will not rest. He does not sleep, and he is breathless after talking.

She asks the eunuch to make sure that he is given mashed fish, honey in lemon water, and the broth of a chicken boiled with fresh herbs. She feeds him herself while he works away. When he does sleep she watches him thrash and talk of his mother, of his father—not Zeus but Phillip.

She does not have to think hard about the one he misses and still mourns. He has had a fine monument built in his memory, and had it lit. It burned so bright that many folk saw it. And he asked the people of Egypt to give him the title of a demi-god. For in Egypt all Kings are Gods and as King of Egypt, Alexander has the power to invest this honour upon the one that loved him the most. But they have refused him.

He drinks more wine. To relieve the pain he also takes the black paste of the poppy. More and more of it.

Work, work, work, until the sweat falls like a river from his body. Then the intense cold, followed by anger, wine and sleep.

When he wakes his mouth is coated in dried spit, his breath fetid and he is always disorientated.

The day arrives when the guards on the Ishtar gates announce the arrival of representatives from the House of Antipater, the great saviour of the United States of Greece.

Alexander is carried out in a litter to greet the party. But it is not Antipater that leaps from a horse in the front of the line of military men, but Cassander, his son.

Alexander's shock is noticeable, so Ptolemy steps forward and hugs the man. A boy who shared their

teaching school with them. Whom Aristotle also poured
wisdom upon. But Alexander never liked the boy. He was
smug and devious. He cheated and copied. His father, on
the other hand—never a more honourable chap, but
Cassander, no. A man of no honour and a man whom
Alexander often wished dead.

"Turn me around," Alexander says. He leaves
Ptolemy with the scoundrel.

When they are back in their apartment he rants
and raves. "Call Perdicass," he shouts to the eunuch.

Perdicass is in the court helping direct the staff to
set up the banquet that was planned to welcome
Antipater.

Roxane hears his heavy steps on the staircase, and
opens the door to the panting, oversized general.

"Yes, you called?"

There is no formality anymore. At one time she
would observe how his generals would wait and greet her
husband in a graceful way, familial. But now they tend to
brush him aside and put up with, not listen, to what he has
to say.

"Cassander, the audacity."

"But Alexander, he is younger and fitter than his
father. We have heard that Antipater often is lost in
thought, his mind's not so clear, his words not so
eloquent these days. Therefore who better than his eldest
son to fill the role of the Satrap of Babylon?"

"You knew about this?"

Perdicass waves his fat hand, more like a paw, to
the ill King. "Not really, but we did have some idea
Antipater might not be fit to travel."

"Why was I not told?"

Roxane takes her husband's hand as he shelters
his eyes from the light. "My love, sometimes you are so
ill that you sleep. And you need to sleep to gain your
strength, so that you can continue with your plans. Often

———

193

it is your loyal generals that take the burden of the day to day away from you."

She asks Perdicass to leave.

It is mid-year. The river is low and smells of dead fish and all the waste that rots in it. She shuts the door to keep out the odour. But it is as hot as a frying pan inside, so she asks the eunuch to find some men who would wave some palms in the room, to keep it a little less warm.

They arrive. They are dark men and they smile at her, honoured to be asked to be in the presence of their King. She feels the Babylonians' loyalty, their love for her husband. There is no disdain in them.

She has dressed in a plain, pale-blue chiton for it is too hot to wear her new clothes. She is barefoot and she trickles cold water over her husband to keep him from burning up. This is the third day of a terrible fever. She smells the fever. It reminds her of strong hot urine to which aromatic sour herbs have been added. She asks the eunuch if he might find some sandalwood to burn in the room.

When Alexander falls unconsciousness she tells the eunuch to fetch Ptolemy.

The generals—Ptolemy, Perdicass and Cassander— surround her husband. His eyes are shut and his breath is raspy. She sits at his head and strokes his hair and his brow. The eunuch sits beside the foot of the bed as many of the Greek soldiers file through. No one speaks. Candles and incense burn. The doors are open and a slight breeze moves through the room.

For a moment Alexander rouses, turns to her and says that the Kingdom should go to the strongest. She knows who the strongest is.

Perdicass smiles. He touches his ring. Ptolemy walks out onto the balcony and Cassander leaves the room.

Once again her husband is lying, waiting. Perhaps he waits for recovery, perhaps he waits for death. She does not know. But she takes the time to think, of Craterus taking charge, regrouping, stabilising some part of this kingdom without complexity. Retreating even from the enormity of what her husband has created. She thinks of the boy she carries within. How he can grow up in the presence of man who swore a solemn oath. That of a soldier loyal to Alexander, loyal to the Macedonian crown.

She thinks of Andronicus and his talk of the soft blue sea, the waves that lapped upon the shore that sat below his family home. The orchards, the plentiful food, the gentle climate. She sees a dark-haired boy ride a horse, much like his father rode a horse, with confidence and with great skill. A hunter, like herself, like his father. A man who fights well in battle. Who will be mentored by the strongest.

He dies. Roxane leans over him and kisses him. His lips are dry. She shuts his eyes. He looks so young again, so peaceful. She smooths down his blond hair.

All of a sudden there is a banging, a noise, shouting. This is not how it should be. She cannot see clearly for the turbulence. There is fighting and soldiers, their sandals clapping loudly on the tiled floor. And then there is darkness. Someone has placed a hood over her head, and arms are wrapped around her.

She is being carried downstairs and out into the fresh air, down a road, for she hears the donkeys braying and the noise of the Babylonians who wail. And then she is through a door. The scent of the river is strong and then the door is closed and she is being taken down, down into something that is still and sheltered. There is a deafening peace now, a quiet.

The Forge 322 BC

Outside I play with the flame that gathers and sustains my forge. It is a good fire, a good flame and I have taught young Benjamin the art of metal work, the art of making fine things. And for that I am pleased.

The death of Alexander has brought with it unrest. In the streets large gangs of soldiers patrol. The street vendors have disappeared. The colour of the city has faded to what seems a deep, dull grey.

Beulah tells me not to worry. To ride it out. This is the nature of this city. She will rise again and she will become again a beauty.

We sit in the courtyard and drink to the flame. For what is left to toast. Our business is simmering, as Beulah puts it—wait, be patient and our customers will return.

"Do you think of her, Andronicus?"

"Who?"

"Of the Queen, of the beautiful woman we dressed, and her child."

"No."

"I think of her all the time. The gossips say that as soon as Alexander died, she stole a horse and rode to the House of Susa where she slaughtered the living wives of Alexander and any child she thought might have been born to them."

I laugh.

"You don't believe this?"

"No."

"Well what do you think happened to her?"

"They would have killed her; she carried the heir. These generals and not generals scrap now over the leftovers of a kingdom."

I have seen men, mercenaries, join the ranks of the rebels. I have seen Ptolemy strut as if he is in charge. I have seen Cassander give orders to men to murder any dissidents who question his authority. I have seen men spit on the memorial site where Hephaestion's star burned bright.

I believe that fat Perdicass sits in the throne room, thinking he has inherited the kingdom. He believes Alexander left it all to him. I have heard that the great Peucestas now thinks of himself as a Persian noble. And that the eunuch so loyal to his master threw himself in the river and drowned. The stories differ, but basically no one can dispute that the Greek men are vying for control of whatever is ripe for the picking.

"And where do you think Alexander's body is?"

"Talk on the street is that they cut it into pieces and fed it to the hungry dogs."

"Barbaric."

"Yes, quite."

I take more of her strong drink, for it takes all thought away and helps me sleep.

It is a day typical of these times. Benjamin makes a little stock to hold in reserve, mainly the bracelets. They are quite a novelty in the city and further afield, and many come with memories that need to be preserved in an article so solid it will never disappear. Some come in remembrance of loved ones that passed. A boy died of a fever, but he loved his pet rabbit, he loved the fish in the river. He was partial to a pear. And so we craft these miniature items and fasten them with one ring to the chain of many rings.

Gold is more popular than silver. Today we make up only the chain and the clasps.

Our box, made out of tin painted black and gold, holds enough coins. And we have stored more of the same behind the bricks in the room where I sleep.

We tap and fiddle and polish. The door opens, which now is rare.

It is General Ptolemy. I feel a sickness deep down in my stomach. I wish to be anonymous in this town, but of course he knows my name. And he calls me this morning, "Andronicus, son of Nicodemus".

I wipe my hands and ask what I can do for him.

He is silent a long while and then says, "Shall we go outside?"

I take him to the light. My light, my forge. The friend of fire.

He sits in a chair and I stand by my fire. "Andronicus—I have a proposal."

I nod.

"Tomorrow we move. Back to our homeland. Cassander, Perdicass and I are planning to strike out from Babylon tomorrow and hit the road back to the land of our birth. I would very much like it if you would join my unit."

"For what?"

"For the purposes of protection."

I am stunned. I am not a guard, nor a soldier. I have no combat skills. But then of course I realise that I am the son of an arms maker.

"Meet me at dawn by the Ishtar gates, and from there one of my men will give you your instructions."

That night I tell Beulah and Benjamin that I am to leave.

"But why?" Beulah says.

"Orders."

"But you are now one of us. All Babylon is full of people who have created their own identity, like us. We are able to be who we like, when we like. You must stay. You have built such a following, you are wealthy, and you have taught Benjamin much. You are family, Andronicus."

I feel pain. I do not want to leave but I have no choice.

"Benjamin is more than able to run the workshop on his own. He must use the wealth we have accumulated to buy great gems, set gems now into his bracelets, fit a pearl and with gold as his friend, turn it into the mythical white bear of the north. There is much scope. People love anything miniature."

I steal the words of Zek. It seems so long ago now that we met the silk trader. I no longer have the talisman he gifted me for it was swept away in the great rain that turned into a river.

"I must go. It was not a request, Beulah, but an order."

"Why? Just resist, disobey."

I shake my head. I point to the little cobbled lane to the west of us. To the scribe's small doorway. "Did you not see what they did to old Leander?"

Beulah's eyes start to fill. I continue with my reasoning. "He was asked to take some notes for Ptolemy. He did so, but when Ptolemy asked him to be his resident scribe, he refused and shut his door. That night Ptolemy's thugs came and burned his home. They burnt to death not only Leander but his new Babylonian wife and their child."

Beulah holds my hand.

"This will happen if I don't obey, and you will lose everything. I am not going to do this to you or your family. Benjamin with your fine work, and Beulah, you are the best seamstress I have ever known. When your husband returns with your daughter you will be able to show him what you have achieved in his absence and then he will be able to craft fine sculptures and statues that will adorn this city, which is in need of rebuilding."

The dawn is sharp, the breeze of a winter not far off. I wait and admire those gates. Such beauty in the blue of them set with gold figures. The marduks, the lions, the stars. It is all such a wonder. I sink my eyes into them and do not think about what lies before me.

Then after some time, my mind wanders. What will I find there? I think my father will be dead. My mother possibly still lives. She will be elderly, perhaps, and she will need help with our land. Who is in charge in Macedonia? I hope Craterus is in the palace. They say he is helping the dim-witted half-brother of Alexander to manage the throne. I will make small arms again to furnish Ptolemy's regiment.

I have taken very little with me. I do not want the burden of carrying anything heavy. I am too old to haul great carts or bags around with me. I wear just one gold bangle and one gold ring.

Ptolemy directs his guard to me. The guard is dressed in fine military attire. Black and red. The new colours of the House of Ptolemy.

"Wait here," the guard tells me, "and soon you will see what it is we need you to do."

Cassander's men are further out from the gates of Babylon. They drill and perform in their new regalia. Purple and dull silver. Tan leather. I wonder about the unpolished silver but then perhaps it is deliberate, for the sun will not catch on it and this will make them less exposed.

Perdicass left a few days ago; his small army is ahead of these two larger groups of soldiers.

It seems he is to take charge of the throne room at the palace.

I am weary with these thoughts, which are speculative and exhausting. I am resigned now to do whatever it is they want in the hope that they will leave me in alone in Macedonia.

A horn sounds. Three shrill blows. And then the gates open. Before my eyes passes a glass-sided wagon drawn by white horses, all dressed in the purple of Kings. On the wagon is the body of our late King; although his face is a mask, it is clearly the face of Alexander. The body is sealed somehow and wrapped in strips of fine gold silk. And around this kind of shrine are fresh flowers and laurel leaves. Behind his cortege a figure comes. She is dressed in a pale blue chiton and she is riding on a small ass. She carries in her arms a child. The child is dark with curly hair.

The guard whispers to me that I have been assigned to march beside Roxane. She has asked specifically that I be her guardian.

On The Road 322 BC

She sees the sea for the first time and is delighted. It is the first time I have seen light come into her eyes; the first time she even speaks to me. Up until now she has remained silent.

The boy is enchanting, his smile delightful. He giggles and sleeps well. He feeds from his mother. She carries with her one soft cotton bag with three light blue chitons.

"What happened to the clothes we made for you?"

"I do not know, Andronicus." She inhales. "I do – not – know."

One night she sidles up to me, very close. She whispers, "Andronicus, did you notice that Cassander's campsites are getting further away?"

I had not noticed. "What do you make of this?"

She turns her head so no one can see her lips. "I think we are slowing down, putting more distance between ourselves and Cassander."

She is tired. Her cheeks are sunk, and her hair is streaked with grey. "I will try to sleep," she says.

A few days later we are told to take some rest. Another day passes and still we do not move. The talk is that we are waiting for supplies.

We ease into a gentle kind of routine. I hold the child, which she calls Alexi, when she is in need of privacy; to dress, to toilette. I have grown fond of him.

He is unlike most children I have come across due to his
conviviality. We talk little, and the awkwardness that
plagued us at first has now grown into a kind of
contentment. We both enjoy the landscape—it's a
peaceful place in which we enjoy a sustaining silence.

There was a small commotion this morning. We shuffle a
little here and there; the wagons are checked and turned.
The cortege is refreshed with foliage, and we are told to
exercise the horses. Roxane leads them around and
around this space. We try to find out what's happening,
then orders come from up the line that we are to take an
angle best favoured for the next stage of our travel.
Guards direct us into our new positions and then we
slowly start to move again.

This night it is clear, the moon large in the sky and she
once again seeks me out as I sit with my back against the
wheel of her husband's wagon. "Do you see the moon?"
she asks.

"Yes, she is fine tonight."

"Where is she in the sky?"

I look up and she sits in the west.

Then she points to the north star, the bright
guiding light. "It was in front of us, Andronicus. Now it is
behind us."

She closes her eyes. "We have somehow changed
direction. I think Ptolemy has changed direction; slowly
he has turned us round. For the sea today was on our
right, not on our left."

I had not noticed.

"There are no signs of the campsites of
Cassander."

"Why would he do that?"

She shrugs her shoulders and cradles her sleeping child. "Why do anything?"

It is as though she is defeated. She is lost without Alexander, or any of his men that were loyal to her. The eunuch is gone; Craterus, who she was fond of, is back in Macedonia. She has no one—no one but me.

I feel a pang of guilt. I sit with her, and in the bright light of the nearly full moon, she begins to speak again.

"I have never been so frightened," she says. "The night Alexander died, when I should have sat with him until he cooled. When I should have been able to discuss his funeral with his friends." She takes a sip of wine. "Instead I was taken by force and placed in a sealed room. I thought I would die there. There was no food or water."

"Where were you? Did you know?"

She shakes her head. "No, not at first, but it was very dry and warm and I thought I must have been somewhere under the ziggurat. In a kind of buried room. They say that under the ziggurat is the fire of eternity. The dragon lives there, and his breath heats the water of the town."

She sips again and places her finger inside a curl on her son's forehead. She unwinds it and the curl springs back. "Then, not long after I started to think about my impending death, there was a noise outside the locked door and hooded guards brought the dead body of Alexander in. He was wrapped in a heavy blanket. They laid him down. Not long after that a team of men came. One of the men's faces was painted green. He carried a staff and wore a tail. At first they seemed fierce, but they weren't, not at all. They brought with them many bags and baskets and set up a table.

"While I waited for the birth, they prepared my husband in death. I was fed well, but we fasted every other day. They spoke a little Greek. They took all the insides out of my husband and cleaned his carcass out with rags. They anointed him in oils and placed him first in a salt bath and then in a bath of fresh sawdust. Then after some time they rubbed him in wax and wrapped him in the gold that he wears now. They placed a mask upon his desiccated face."

She places Alexi on her wrap in the grass. She puts a finger to her lips. "And then I felt my son coming. I dreaded this, for my births usually ended up with a dead child. So I thought, well here they are, ready to take his body and make him like his father. They will place our son beside his father and they will make him into a kind of statue too.

"He did not dally, this Alexi. He arrived fast and it was the Egyptian embalmers that helped me. They caught him, cut the cord of his birth string. They were jubilant."

I look to the south. "Perhaps they have decided that you all belong in the new palace. That it's a good place for you to be until Alexi is older."

"Perhaps," she says.

"Maybe you will sail instead to Greece. It is a fine sea that rims these lands. You will make a grand entrance on a boat."

"I would like to see dolphins and other sea creatures and collect some shells."

Alexandria 322 BC

We are separated, all of us. When we reach Memphis in Egypt, they unhitch the cortege and leave Alexander there, telling us that a shrine is to be built in the Alexandria, the new city, and in time he will be moved.

They take Roxane and her child. She is bundled into a covered wagon; it is quite rudimentary. The guards who take her do not use kind or polite language. They are rough with her. It happens so suddenly that I don't have time to think of anything. I should have intervened, saved her.

I am told to walk with a band of men who gather. It seems once again I am a civilian trailing behind the military men. They are foreigners: Cyrus of Persia, Nicodemus of Sparta, Parsu of Phoenicia.

We converse in simple Greek. With the few words that Cyrus knows, he tells us he is a carpet weaver. Parsu, a glass maker.

"A group of artisans," I say more to myself than anyone else.

We arrive at the palace gates, but not at the main gates, and we are escorted to a courtyard. Each one of us is shown to a small workshop. In my room is a set of silver smithing tools. Behind the main table where I will work is a partition behind which is a pallet bed.

I walk out into the Alexandrian sunshine to find that there are many men stationed here: guards on the gates, a florist in the centre, a jeweller in one corner, a brush maker, a potter.

I find a communal forge in the back quarter, manned by many boys. There is a good healthy fire which will be adequate—I know already that I am to work in silver, for on my bench is a bag of silver with the various metals to give an article strength. Someone has drawn up designs of platters, sconces and candlesticks.

I am sent a team of men, all Egyptians who work with metal.

Elissa is my only contact with the palace that looms above us. She is Carthaginian and proud of it. She speaks our tongue, and presents me each day with our assignments. She weighs our silver and metal before it is smelted and moulded, polished and tweaked and then she weighs the finished articles and enters her results on a pad of fine parchment.

Our days are with the light, and after that we all gather for an evening meal which is supplied. We sit at wooden tables under the cover of an awning; we struggle to find conversion for we are all tired. The wine gives us pause to rest a little, but it is not the fine wine of Greece, it's a watery red slop of what might be anything—a fruit, a herb, a root vegetable. It is the only thing that cheers us despite its horrific taste.

As I go on making these things to furnish the new palace, my curiosity wanes to a point where I become resigned and almost content.

I have food, shelter and a bed. The work is not too tedious and sometimes I am able to wrangle the drawn design so that I can place a little of myself in the piece. An odd etched fish, a little worm I am able to craft and fix on the lip of a drinking vessel. This becomes my amusement.

So this is how I am to spend my days. I will live like this until this old heart stops beating.

I do not allow myself to think of the past. There are too many regrets, too many times when I could have made life better for myself and those who were in my care. I could have insisted that with my father's gold, we should have turned back at Troy. But such is life. The Fates decide. And it is my fate now to grow old. To honour my given talent, that of a silversmith. Isn't that really what my father was? Oh, he worked in other metals too, but it was a simple task of providing something of purpose, a useful item. Not an item to be purely decorative, to convey a certain status on a person. So he was right in the end. There is a labour we are born to. My lot was always to turn something dug from the ground into an article of purpose.

My father knew this but I had my head turned towards a golden kingdom that never came to fruition.

I do not dwell on this. Instead I nod with my new friends. We discuss only the sea of Alexandria. It has moods, this sea, and one time in the year it grows wild and the sea spray rains over us and we feel a renewed enthusiasm for our work.

I do not assume anything. Our appointed representatives are no doubt sworn to keep the secrets of the palace. Old Parvu did once ask his rep boy who occupied the palace above. The boy merely said the King and Queen of Egypt.

So Ptolemy lives above, with Thais. This is my conclusion. Roxane may be back in Pella by now. Her son too.

The Coat 310 BC

This day is long, and I am feeling the ache of age in my fingers, the creak of my knees, the pain in my hips. I soldier on, that is what I call it now. A duty to the state and a time to regard all things as basic. The basic workmanship of turning silver and their alloys into functional yet beautiful pieces. Isn't that what I always wanted?

To see my face in a polished piece and know that the lines on my face tell many tales. Tales that I tell to myself in the most silent ritual each night as I beg sleep to come upon me.

I walk each day, surveying the young boys who work the large communal forge, smelling the sea and then spying her curves as she changes from season to season. I walk to the gate most days curious to know what other procurements are gracing these iron posts and these surly guards.

One guard is remonstrating with an old hag at the eastern gate. We get beggars, and those who are hungry call here in the hope that we might have something spare to give them.

This woman will not give up. She speaks little Greek—a few words, but I hear two that make me stop in my tracks.

"Roxane, Queen," she repeats. She is flanked by an odd man, who limps and does not speak much at all. He bobs his head and has a curved back. I move over to them asking if I can help.

The old woman nods, she is very short and very round. "Roxane, she must have this." She shows me a piece of brown clothing. "Mother. Dead."

I start to form some kind of picture in my head. A brown coat that Roxane's mother wore, trimmed with fur. She spoke of it. How her mother was so cold that the other wife of Oxyartes made her a coat to wear.

"Give her, please. Mother's wish. Now mother dead. We walk long way."

The boy nods. "Roxane, must have. Lei-la. Dead. Lei-la cry that … Roxane must have coat."

"Dying wish," the little round woman says. "Very important dying wish done."

She heaves the coat over the gate to the guard, who holds it far from him, as though it is a dying dog. I take it from him and turn to the woman who has already disappeared.

"Well, Andronicus." The guard smiles and takes it from my hands. "Better check for knives and any other dangerous thing that might be stashed in the hem and seams." He feels it and is quite satisfied that nothing lives in its inner folds. "There you go. Good luck getting it to her. I believe that she is hidden somewhere no one will find her. The boy attends the academy, I believe. Maybe it would be best to try there first."

The only person that can help me deliver the coat is Elissa, so when the workshop is empty and she is totting up the final weights in her ledger, I approach her. I peel off my ring and bangle, quite surprised they are still on my person, that nobody has come claiming them as some sort of tax or payment for my keep. I lay them in front of her and she raises her dark eyes to me. "Andronicus, a gift, for me. How kind."

"More payment for a favour you might be able to do for me."

She rolls up the parchment, secures it with the purple ribbon and places her head in her hands. She looks tired. "What can I do for you?"

I remove the folded-up coat from the shelf beneath my workbench and place it in front of her. She does not look impressed.

"This coat, it was the coat of Roxane's mother. And it was her mother's dying wish that she should have this coat. I know it doesn't look much, but I guess it contains the scent of her mother, memories of a time when they both lived in the north, a place known for its bitter winters. I can testify to that." I know I am rambling, so I stop. I wait and then go on. "I wish to get this to her."

Elissa feels the brown wool, teases out the fur that is matted and knotty on the hood. "Upstairs is a place that Thais presides over. She is like a hawk, Andronicus. Everything, but everything up there is accounted for. Informants lurk in the shadows waiting to catch anyone who even looks at a morsel of food or dares to sit on a bench to bask in the sun for a few moments."

"But all I am asking is that this coat be given to Roxane."

"I believe she is held in a tower on the eastern side, under guard."

"What about her son?"

"I don't know about her son."

"What if you were to give this to the guard who watches her?"

"That is out of bounds for me, Andronicus. I walk up those stairs there –" she points to the back stairs, "then I give your finished items to the stores master. I hand over my scroll to another man who sits on a high stool counting all day, and then I walk out a side door to help the kitchen staff chop and cut vegetables and fruit. Once I am done with that I am allowed to go back to our mother's house. But before the guard will open the eastern gate for me, I am checked. Patted down and poked to make sure I have stolen nothing. If I was to stray out of my area I would be asked to leave."

"So you work in the kitchen in between doing this job here."

"Yes, not one minute of my time here is wasted. Queen Thais makes it the same for all of us. You down here have it quite good, Andronicus. Look at my hands, nothing more that puffed up red skin and cuts everywhere."

I hold mine out to her—the black-rimmed nails of a smith, the burn scars, the wound scars. We laugh.

"We get wine," I say.

"We get a few coins each week with which my mother buys bread and a bit of meat. She has just enough left over to pay the landlord."

The next afternoon when it is just us, Elissa comes to me. "I had an idea and I discussed it with my sister. She cleans on the floor below where she thinks Roxane is held. She says she will help you; she will create some sort of distraction where you might be able to climb the steep staircase and hand the coat over to the guard."

Elissa begins to draw out the layout on the table before me, using chalk. She whispers and says, "Tomorrow at this time. I will let you out into the corridor and my sister will be waiting."

I take off my gold again. But she pushes it away. "It's all on you, Andronicus. If we get caught you must deny that my sister and I had anything to do with it, and I can tell you, you will be lucky to pull it off."

The next day after we finish work, I follow Elissa up the back stairs. She takes the store master's hand and places it down her top. Then she scolds the accountant, "What are looking at? You want a turn? Well it will cost you, just like it costs him." Elissa pulls a small curtain closed.

I slide in and out of that narrow room and into the corridor. I see a girl there, in the shadows, with a cleaning cloth and broom. She nods and we walk down the vast hallway. We see people and she greets them with a small whisper. "A new servant, about to be put to task." She begins a spiel about how this must be done. Dry dust, wet dust and then clean cloth to dry the wet. See, three things. The polishes, all of them, are kept up ahead in the cupboard to the left.

We reach the cupboard; every shelf is filled with jars of wax and oils. She pushes me in. Shuts the door. I have the coat under my chiton, held firm with a leather belt. She checks to make sure no one else is in the cupboard before she speaks. "Now go down to the left and then turn and go straight ahead. At the end you will come across a set of stairs, go up there. I think that is where she is."

My heart is racing. *Think, think.* The whole idea of it all is making me sick.

As we separate, I hear in my wake her shrill voice. "Hey, who did this section? Bennu, you lazy mule, did you not hear what I said this morning? That this whole section was to be mopped three times? You need to see yourself in the floor, and if you don't you keep mopping and drying until you do."

I hear the patter of feet. More than one; she has staged a small meeting of what must be the people who work under her. So I run.

I find the stairs and clamber up them.

There is guard sleeping in the chair. His lips are stained red; his jug is empty. He snores loudly. I look into the room he sits outside. The door is open.

Inside is a place not fit to house even the mangiest dog. There is a slops bucket still full. The dust is thick. The bedroll is old and unwashed. In front of me the balcony is open with no windows to close should a breeze come up. The roof is open at one end.

"What do you want?"

I turn and the guard rises unsteady on his feet.

"I have been ordered to give this to Roxane, the woman who resides here."

"A woman? She is more like a stray cat. But you are too late, she was fetched before dawn and she and her boy were put on a boat. Just down there."

I follow his finger out to the bay, where there is a jetty to the left of the palace. "Yep, I watched 'em board a boat myself. Fishing boat, I think. Watched them sail away. And then someone comes and says, 'enjoy your wine.' They place a pitcher in my hand and then tell me when I am finished, to leave."

I watch him, in his drunken state, wipe his eyes. "And I been here guarding this place for many a time. I don't get any thanks. Just some scraps to eat, like her. But I sit and do nothing so I think this is a good job. Nice and easy. But now. No home, no place to go. At least she used words that were not offensive. In a way I felt sorry for her. I heard her say like proper Greek language, not like the words I was raised with. Crude like and loud like. She used these phrases that were gentle and like a story. I used to listen to her talk to herself. She talked to the sea out there. Called it her friend."

I touch his upper arm. I say thank you.

"What for?"

"For telling me what happened to her."

"It's nothing. I mean, what else could I tell her? Another meanness of the Queen, eh—she sends you with a warm coat. Well, couldn't she have done with that from the time they put her in here? Just another little joke that she thinks is funny."

As I descend I hear him sit back down in his chair with a groan.

When I reach the bottom I look down the hall, towards the sea, and I see that the end door is wide open. I put on the coat, the hood over my head, my hands in its deep pockets, and I walk down that hallway and out the door. It is dark, the sun has gone and the storm's call has begun. The thrash of the waves, the hurl of its spray, the wind whining in the hollows of the building. I hide behind the trees, behind the small buildings and I run down to the shore. I climb over the big rocks there and hurry on and on, following the shoreline, past the jetty and into the small harbour area.

I walk then, walk and walk. I do not stop.

Across The Sea 310 BC

Roxane doesn't mind the slow lilt of the ocean. She shares her gaze of the deep blue sea with that of her son. The sea, her son. How good they both are. He is dark, tall, handsome. With her green eyes.

The boat smells of fish and the captain and crew do not speak much. It is a perfect harmony. She feels the sun as its sheds its light on them. They have left behind the storm.

"We were tied up, our hands were tied, Alexi, when they brought us to this boat, but now we are here on board, we are free." She feels her wrists where the guards that collected her bound her hands with rope.

"My uncle has at last honoured what is really mine, ours."

"Your uncle?"

"King Ptolemy. At last he is sending me back to take my place, to finish what my father started."

"Ptolemy—I do not believe he is your uncle."

"He is my father's half-brother."

"The only uncle whose life was spared by your grandmother was Arrhidaeus. I think Olympias only saved him from death because he was not of good mind. And I believe you are called back now by Craterus, for Arrhidaeus is either dead or near dead."

She touches him. He is awkward as her hands smooth his hair, pat his skin, but he allows it for she looks so ill. She is bone. She has gone grey. Although he was not allowed to leave the academy, his door was locked and he was guarded always, he did not go without what he needed. He was placed at the academy under guard, his uncle said, because he was a target for assassination.

But his mother—what did they do to her? When he asks, she says only that she is with the sea, she made friends with the sea. "Craterus will now look after us, Alexi," she says. She seems to repeat this most days. These phrases about the sea and about Craterus, and because she seems to rally at the mention of the general's name, Alexi is reluctant to tell her the truth.

She sees dolphins. She sits on the bow with her feet crossed and marvels at them. "See, Alexi, the bearers of truth. The ones who save men."

It is then that he knows he must tell her. For the truth is salvation. It was she who taught him this long ago, and since then he has upheld that value. Always the truth, never a lie.

"Mother, Craterus is dead. I do not know if Arrhidaeus is dead. But I do know that Craterus died."

His mother is suddenly still. She grabs his wrist. Her fingers are strong. Her nails are uncared for. The skin around one nail is ripped and bleeding.

"How did he die?"

"He was killed by Perdicass. You see, there was a rift between Cassander's men and Craterus'. Perdicass sided with Cassander and Perdicass killed Craterus with a knife. Cassander is now in charge in our homeland."

"All my tears are in the ocean," she says. "The tears of my God, the one true god, are what makes the ocean. His sadness, and grief, and I have given him all my tears."

They make landfall late one afternoon. The captain does not row them ashore till just before dawn the next day. When he pulls the boat up on the small sandy beach,

Roxane sees a group of men dressed in black capes. They remind her of ravens.

Then they all walk, these black birds and Roxane and Alexi, out into the countryside. They come to a small house set in an apple orchard.

"You will remain here, for safety reasons. We will come tomorrow when you have had some rest."

Alexi goes to reply, to place his hand in that of the man who spoke, but he says only, "Tomorrow." He opens the door; they walk in and they hear him leave and lock the door behind him.

The fire is lit in the room, a copper kettle is filled with water and a basket sits on the small wooden table. Inside the basket are apples, cheese, bread and wine.

Alexi eats. Roxane takes very little but drinks wine, which soon sends her to sleep. She curls up on one of the narrow beds. When she is asleep Alexi places a blanket over her, tucking it about her so that she does not get cold.

He tries to recall Roxane before they were separated. They lived in the big palace for a while, in a wing away from the Ptolemies. His memories are sketchy. He doesn't even remember the day that his tutor, John, took him to the academy to live. John, who cried when they came for him. John, who mused about many things and inspired him to open his mind. "Open up your mind, Alexi …" And when he was too tired to think anymore, it was John who would say, "Well, let us do something different, like playing dice, and once you have softened your mind to a task that you like, it will allow you then to take a deeper corridor and you will wander down this thought portal and you will find the answer has been there all along."

With John's assistance and guidance, he learnt languages, studied the cosmos, dissected animals, planted small trees and many other botanicals. He was made to draw these plants and leaves, so that he would become a master at drawing and using the pen to illustrate thought. He was to recite *The Iliad* and *The Odyssey*.

They never really socialised with anyone. His cousins, all red-headed and loud, would be dismissed at noon and allowed to ride horses and play games.

Alexi learned to ride and hunt, but it was always indoors in the vast, covered indoor arena, for John said he was a much-valued man. Many wanted him dead.

Yet here he is, in this house, about to be officially announced as the true heir to the Macedonian crown.

John said it was better to rule a small and gifted nation than to try to take on more lands. Where your blood is, where your forebears were born, is the land on which you must make great again. But Alexi hankers after the sights his father saw, the people he talked with. The nations he opened up.

It is not dawn, and there is a rap at the door. It's not a friendly rap. Roxane is already up and she gazes out the small window. "Grass," she says.

Alexi rises from his bed and tussles his hair. It is thick and annoying if not cut often. He walks to the door as the key turns in the lock.

A man, dressed like the men yesterday in a black-hooded cape, enters. Behind him follow more men dressed the same.

The man with the scroll clears his throat before unfurling the parchment. He reads: "Alexander, born in Babylon, paternity unknown, you are charged with treason and this is punishable by death."

Roxane turns from the window. She stares at the man. "This is the son of King Alexander, the true heir."

———

Alexi's face reddens. He cannot move. He cannot speak.

"We believe that you, Roxane of Sogdia, did lie about the nature of your relations with Alexander the Great and for this and your deception you are to be hung as well."

Alexi, in fury, steps forward. He hits the scroll with his fingertip. The men behind the old crow pull out knives.

"And what treason am I charged with? And how can you doubt my mother? She never uses a lie."

The crow man continues. "Alexander born of Babylon, you were heard plotting with your tutor about setting up an army and naval base in Massalia. You were heard to say, you would invade Macedonia from the west."

Alexi laughs. "Every few days I had a lesson in strategic geography. Many times it was from a military defence and offence perspective; sometimes it was from a cropping or supply angle, and yes we did discuss the advantages of a place like Massilia. But this was a teaching exercise, nothing more."

"Well, your uncle has signed a document to the fact that he himself heard you plot the overthrow of Cassander, now ruler of Macedonia."

"I wish to have a meeting with General Cassander."

The man with the scroll continues to read. "Further to that, it is stated that you have voiced dissent and criticised your uncle's leadership in Egypt. That you have been known to say that he is undeserving of the city your father built and founded."

Alexi sits and places his head in his hands and rubs his eyes. He knows that at times when John took him to the great library, and when they watched the harbour develop, that John did let slip his true feelings about the rule of the Ptolemies. That they had seen an opportunity and taken the most lucrative land. They had secured their rule in the time of chaos, and they had made it their own kingdom.

Alexi chooses to be silent.

"And of course we believe you are not descended from royal blood."

Roxane sits beside her son. "He is of much royal blood. That of Cyrus the Great and that of my husband Alexander."

The man rolls up the parchment, places the black ribbon around it. "You will be hanged tomorrow before first light."

The men of Cassander retreat, and as they walk out they nod to a man of grey hair also dressed in dark clothing. He places another basket on the table under the instruction of the head crow.

"Your last meal," the crow says.

The door is locked. The door is bolted.

There is no light tonight. No mother moon to converse with. Roxane takes much wine. Alexi does too. They do not eat.

"It was all arranged."

"Lies are the darkness in the world; now we go to the light," Roxane says.

"We were held as a bargaining tool. A treasure that everyone was wondering about. Now Ptolemy and Thais have exchanged us in return for their exclusive rule of the place my father valued the most. The richest nation on earth. Egypt. Well done to them. And now Cassander has what he wanted all along. The legitimate heir, and he will exterminate me and there will be no more challenges to the throne of Macedonia. What vultures do prey on the

---

remains of my father's lands. I should have been wiser. I should have foreseen this and saved us."

Roxane takes her son's hand. "We will be saved. We will go to the bridge of judgement and we will be flown to the great golden kingdom above. All will be well."

"I could have persuaded the captain on that boat to fake a sinking, so that we would have been able to escape. With all of the world thinking we had drowned we could have gotten away and then mounted some kind of attack when the time was right."

"That would have been a deception. A lie. We would have had to live in hiding. We would have had to find a home."

Just as they lie down on their narrow beds, to try to sleep, to try to hasten the eventual outcome, Roxane hears a soft tap at the door.

The wine has taken Alexi.

She walks towards the door and presses her ear to the wooden panels. "Forgive me," the voice says. "I followed your jailers. I heard a rumour of your arrival. And I needed to speak with you."

"Yes, the door is locked."

"Yes, there is no way to fiddle with it and release you, and even if I could I am only here at this time because the nearest guard has fallen asleep."

"I am Roxane. My son is Alexi."

"Yes, but look, I cannot be long, the guard will wake. They are a keen lot, Cassander's lot, keen and mean. So I say this to you. I leave by the step something that is for you. When he died, I took it. He instructed me to, just in case I should come across you again. It is a token of his love, the oath of a soldier. I leave it where you can feign a slight fall and remove it from the rock under which I will place it now. The rock is to the right of the doorway."

Roxane calls out some more. But the voice has disappeared. She closes her eyes and sees many rocks. The Sogdian rock, on which they lived, the rock with the shell imprint and small white bones of the fish. The rocks that she used to set out for Alexi when he was small, pretending they were battlefields so she could show her son how brilliant her husband was when it came to overcoming a more powerful enemy.

The dawn comes. Alexi and his mother are resigned to their fate. Six hooded and cloaked men arrive and open the door. The day is new, the dew sparkles on the green grass and the trees are laden with apples.

She does as the voice told her and slips on the wet grass. She falls and takes from under the rock, unseen and unheard, a ring. It is Craterus' ring. She recognises it as the ring that Alexander gave to his most loyal generals. A token of his love. She places it on her finger, allowing her sleeves to fall down over her hands.

The rope is tight on their necks. The executioners are to work in tandem so that both mother and son will perish together. The birds will love these apples. "Please," she whispers to the man on the end of the rope, "please leave us to hang amongst the apples."

Nico has hidden in the shadows. He looks away as the bodies start to swing. He watches the executioners fold up their tools. He hears Cassander's main man say to the executioner nearest to him, "Let the bodies remain until night fall. A deterrent to any other arrogant pretender to the throne."

Nico appears when the crows and executioners are well gone. It is still early and the road outside the orchard

———

225

is quite empty. He prays it will remain so for just a few moments more.

He walks out on the limestone pathway and whistles. A wagon appears out of a glade of willowy trees. A white haired man holds the reins. He is clothed in the simple leather garb of a man who works the land. His tray is loaded up with loose hay.

They work quickly together, Nico and this man. They cut down the bodies and carry them over their shoulders to the wagon where they hide them under the hay.

The driver turns the wagon and the horse moves swiftly down the road away from Pella and the folk who fear Cassander and his tyrannical ways.

They ride up into the mountains; it is a long day. Nico lives some of his time under the peak of Olympus. The rest he walks back to his small home in Pella where he tends to the grave of his former master and friend. He listens to the talk that comes from the court as he walks up and down on the city streets, and then he returns to his peaceful home far away from the unfortunate new age of Greece. He sits at night in his small hut and is warmed by a blazing fire. He eats simply, cooked beans and fish caught in the small river that runs nearby.

They pass his small abode and the wagon driver urges the sturdy large horse further up the mountainside.

Halfway to the top, he stops, and the two men climb down. This man whistles now and his tune reverberates around the rocks and valleys of this mountain.

Seven sons, all brothers, appear and they take the bodies. They wash them using fine white linen cloth and basins which hold the cool clear water of this mountain stream. Then they wrap them in pale blue linen. They walk further up the mountain until they come to a small clearing.

Here they set Roxane and Alexi down on the soft mossy ground. They unwrap them, taking away the cloth.

Nico then gathers stones and places them around the bodies. The boys gather foliage, white flowers that grow wild and decorate the spaces between the stones.

The father closes his eyes. The boys sing a song that they learnt at the knee of their now dead mother. Nico regards the ring on Roxane's hand. For his master did love her the most.

Pay The Ferryman 307 BC

I'm very old now, and I wait to die. The day I left the palace in Alexandria I walked and walked. After three days and nights of following the Nile's pathway south I finally stopped to rest and took shelter under a bush. I slept for just a night and a day before resuming my journey, which took me to the southern temples that sit on the banks of the Nile. I never tire of being here, although I am tired of living.

I watch the ibis and wonder about their holiness. For the priests have told me they are holy birds that rid the earth of evil serpents. They are Thoth, they tell me, the God of the moon, the God of wisdom and it is Thoth that rows Ra's boat across the sky at night so that Ra might bring the light of day to the world.

The night is hot. When I first came here I built myself a hut made only of sticks, much like a hut a Greek bridegroom makes for his new wife on their wedding day. I survive on the generosity of the priests who bring me bowls of stew and the odd passing boat that throws a fish my way. I still kindle a good fire.

I try to sleep, this night. But I cannot get comfortable. My old bones ache and the coat that I use as a blanket is too hot. So I place the old brown coat under me and I stretch out as far as my hut will allow me to.

There is a stone on the ground under the coat, it presses into my ribs. I am tired, but I get up for this nuisance must be found if I'm to get any rest, any peace. I scrabble around in the dust, but there is no stone.

I take the coat. It has become very worn. In the lining the old lady, Muni, had put wool wadding, but much of that has flattened out to nothing and the fur that lines the cuffs and hood is threadbare.

I hold the coat, pressing it, in case a stone has lodged and caught in its old bones—old bones, like my bones. The deep brown of it is like my leathery old skin, which has seen too much life.

My fingers press against a little lump; a nut, perhaps. I take out my knife and prise the material open in the hope that the offender will fall out.

It does, but it is no stone, nor nut, but a five-pointed star. I rise and go to my lamp to get a better look at it. One side is smooth but on the other is a small scene. An etched scene in which there is a mountain, a valley, a river, a tree, and the rippling waves of the sea. Three gems sit above the mountain like stars.

I had a star like this once. From someone. I cannot remember. My mind wanders into places I have been, but the details become lost, as if they have been shaded by a cloud.

There is a pain. Not a pain like the star caused me and my ribs, but a sharp pain running through my chest. I look up and out over the dark river.

I think I see an ibis; the ibis is not a bird now, but the face of my mother. A kindly face with soft grey hair and very blue eyes. It is her.

She calls out to me, but I cannot work out what she is saying. I ask her to speak louder for I have grown deaf.

"Pay the ferryman." Yes, that is what she is saying. "Andronicus, pay the ferryman."

I throw the star into the river. It is in the river and my … hand is pressed to my chest. I cannot speak. All I see is light.

Acknowledgements

I have always had a fascination with Alexander the Great and his world. I read and researched for many years, always eager to know more. However, when it came to deciding on a definitive story for this book I chose three books as mentors. So I am very grateful to these historians and these texts.
–   *Alexander the Great*, by Robin Lane Fox (Penguin, 1973)
–   *Alexander of Macedon, 356-323 B.C.* by Peter Green (University of California Press, 1991)
–   *The Nature of Alexander the Great*, by Mary Renault (Penguin Books, 2001)
–

        I am also so grateful to Sue Copsey who edited my work; to Duncan Barr who carried out my line edit; to Sunè Wiehahn who created my map and made my cover look even more beautiful, to Madeleine Buddo who took the original photograph of my cover, to Kathryn McGarvey who helped me tidy up my digital world, to Sarah Nash who helped me get *World* out into the world and to Florence Charvin who made me look so good.

Key Dates

356 Alexander is born to Phillip and Olympias in Pella
336 Phillip is assassinated
Alexander accedes to the throne
334 Alexander crosses the Hellespont
331 Oracle at Siwah
330 Alexander reaches Persepolis
327 Alexander captures the Sogdian Rock and marries Roxane
326 Alexander defeats Poros at the River Jhelum
Roxane delivers her first child who is still born
326 Alexander is wounded by the Malli on the Indus River
325 Craterus leads the veterans overland
Alexander walks the coastal route
324 Mass weddings take place in Susa
Death of Hephaestion
323 Alexander dies in Babylon
320 The beginning of the Ptolemies reign in Egypt
310 Roxane and Alexander the Fourth are killed by Cassander

Author's note

From the ancient world to the now—
It's not about greed or control; it's about helping those next to you, and honouring and serving the world so that it can nurture everyone born into it.

Other books by Jane Barr:
Cocktails and Peacock Feathers (an anthology of poetry)

Coming soon:
One Cook and Her Travels

Jane Barr is a grandmother to four who loves her family, her friends, her home, navy blue, her trees, champagne and fragrance.

Facebook: @ Jane Barr
Instagram: @Janebarrbooks
Website: www.janebarrbooks.com